Brain Drain

A Salt Mine Novel

Joseph Browning Suzi Yee

Published by Expeditious Retreat Press
Cover by J Caleb Design
Edited by Elizabeth VanZwoll

For information regarding Joseph Browning and Suzi Yee's novels and to subscribe to their mailing list, see their website at https://www.joseph-browning.com

To follow them on Twitter: https://twitter.com/Joseph_Browning

To follow Joseph on Facebook: https://www.facebook.com/joseph.browning.52

To follow Suzi on Facebook: https://www.facebook.com/SuziYeeAuthor/

To follow them on MeWe: https://mewe.com/i/josephbrowning

By Joseph Browning and Suzi Yee

The Salt Mine Novels

Money Hungry
Feeding Frenzy
Ground Rules
Mirror Mirror
Bottom Line
Whip Smart
Rest Assured
Hen Pecked
Brain Drain
Bone Dry
Vicious Circle
High Horse

Chapter One

Bletchley, Buckinghamshire, UK
4th of November, 6:45 p.m. (GMT)

The crew of Bletchley Park Challenge were buzzing around the soundstage. With only fifteen minutes until air, there was still so much to do. To keep them from getting underfoot, the contestants were ushered to the green room as soon as they arrived, an adjacent room with two round tables with four chairs each, a long rectangular table with bottles of water and light snacks, and ample lighting around the mirrors to make sure they were camera ready.

Bletchley Park Challenge was in its fourth season, and was the latest iteration of university quiz shows. Unlike other shows, which were essentially pub quizzes gone highbrow, Bletchley Park Challenge included an element of lateral thinking in addition to raw knowledge recalled at high speeds: the conundrum. Questions were grouped into fives, and the answer to each of those five questions were related in some manner. The team that answered the most questions correctly in that grouping was given the first shot at cracking the conundrum, and points were awarded accordingly. Solving a conundrum delivered half as many points as solving each of the questions that composed it, and conundrums were historically the deciding factor in determining the contest's winner. The format broadened the show's appeal, and Bletchley Park Challenge had launched with high numbers that continued to grow—the last series had almost overtaken the leading UK quiz show.

The concept of mashing up quizzing traditions wasn't new, but it was a stroke of genius on the producer's part to broadcast the show live in Bletchley Park, giving the show both its name and intellectually chic connotations. During the Second World War, the mansion at Bletchley Park had housed the exclusive Government Code and Cypher School responsible for breaking the Enigma and Lorenz ciphers, the two strongest German codes of the time. Deciphering the secret communications of the Nazis was often credited with shortening the war by years, and consequently, many of the Bletchley Park codebreakers had become household names.

Tonight, Leeds University was up against Manchester University, who'd entered the competition to honor Alan Turing, one such codebreaker who had been terribly mistreated because of his homosexuality by the very nation he'd helped preserve. Turing had spent several years at Manchester University's Computing Machine Laboratory after the war, and the connection made them local favorites in the match-up.

The two teams were huddled in their respective corners,

performing their pre-competition rituals and eyeing the competition across the room in their periphery vision. Pre-show jitters ran high, and a pink-haired woman from Manchester University starting tapping her foot as she ran over her mnemonics in her head. At twenty-two years of age, Doris Wood was in her final year of her master's in Evolutionary Biology, and was strong in the sciences and geography but so-so in the humanities. She was quickly becoming a fan favorite after a blazing-hot round in their first appearance, in which she'd correctly answered five conundrums in a row, a feat that had never been done before.

"Would you stop it with the tapping!" her team captain cried out. Asher Leek was one year her junior, but his degrees were stacked against hers. With a master's in Ancient History from the University of Glasgow under his belt, he was currently pursuing his History PhD at the University of Manchester.

"Sorry," Wood responded, and put her hand on her thigh to physically remind her leg not to jostle. She didn't particular care for Leek, but she'd never met anyone that knew as much about history as he did...and with him at the helm, they'd gotten to the finals. Soothed, Leek smoothed back his blond mop of hair in an attempt to regain his composure.

"Don't be a wanker, Leeky," Dylan Black said dismissively. "It's your fault she's twitchy. You're the one that insisted we all knock back two espressos before we go on stage. That's enough to make anyone shaky, much less someone that doesn't drink coffee."

Wood gave her defender, Dylan Black, an appreciative grin. She was a natural smiler, but there was something in her expression that made the twenty-six-year-old student of mathematics and physics return the gesture. Unlike his fellow teammates, he'd already earned degrees at Manchester, but continued his postgraduate studies there instead of at Oxford so he could be closer to his elderly parents who lived in Liverpool.

"It helps us think faster," Leek protested lamely. He hated how young and petulant he sounded in that moment.

"We're not saying that isn't true," Gail Wallace chimed in. "We're saying that you shouldn't be a wanker. The two aren't related." Her dry delivery cut deeper than outright mockery. As a postgraduate student of art history and an ardent pianist, Wallace rounded out the group's knowledge base. She was the oldest of the group—an elderly twenty-eight—and she'd spent much of her youth battling everyone else's opinions about what she and her art should be that she had little patience for unkindness.

"Point taken," Leek conceded, in part because it was so close to show time and winning the tournament was more important to him than this small spat. "I'm sorry," he apologized to Wood and extended an olive branch. "Why don't you pick our first mnemonic?"

Wood was genuinely surprised but recovered graciously and threw out a history mnemonic to the group. "Okay. Let's do the problematic one: English dynasties."

"No Plan Like Yours To Study History Wisely," they repeated in unison. Leek was pleased to see everyone nail it, even Wallace, who struggled with the mnemonic far more than seemed reasonable. It was a short one and made clear sense, but there was something about it that her brain found slippery.

They went clockwise, and Black was next in the circle. "Countries of South America by size," he posed.

"Boring, Average Politics Can Become Very Corrupt. People Everywhere Get Used Sometimes," the group chanted in rhythm. They were moving in sync once again, and they plowed through seven more before the green room door opened.

The stage director took a step into the room to announce, "Ten minutes. Time to find your panel seats, everyone." The screeching sound of eight chairs scraping against the cheap linoleum floor set her hair on end, and she corralled the students while listening in on the chatter on her headset.

The corridor leading backstage was dimly lit, and the bright studio lights momentarily blinded them when they first stepped through the heavy blue curtain onto the stage. Their arrival elicited some cheers from the audience—a crowd of three hundred, with the loudest coming from the friends and family of the contestants. The majority of onlookers were either alumni of the two competing universities or passionate fans of the show.

Seats 154 and 155 were filled by the latter: DCI Simon Jones and his wife, Sarah. Like any good Brit, DCI Jones loved quiz shows, and watching them together had become a tradition now that the kids were out of the house. When he came home from work, they enjoyed cuddling on the couch and watching the daily shows for an hour and a half every night. If he was held up, Sarah would record them for him and they'd catch up whenever time allowed. He was such an avid fan that Monday was DCI Jones's favorite day; primetime quiz shows filled the roster, including Bletchley Park Challenge.

When Sarah had surprised him two weeks ago with tickets to the final, he'd excitedly blurted out that it was the best day of his life. She'd reminded him that he'd had children and was still married—however tenuously at the moment—to which he'd wisely replied, "Second to those, of course. No contest there!"

Once the contestants were settled in, the house lights dimmed and the stage lights kicked on. The background screens lit up and the roaring tympani of the second movement of Beethoven's Ninth Symphony punched into the audience. Code appeared on the screens and dripped down in vertical lines, morphing into mathematical formulas, scientific diagrams, and musical notations. Finally, a montage of important people throughout history flashed on the screen, ending with a picture of Steven Hawking.

Sarah stole a peek at her husband and caught a glimpse of unabashed delight on his face. He was a tenacious and dedicated man in a draining line of work, but in this instant, the years of seeing the worst of humanity on a daily basis faded into the background. She saw the ardent young man who'd won her over thirty years ago, and in that precious moment, she drank her fill of his joy.

As the opening theme music tapered off, the stage lights came up and the dulcet voice of the moderator, Gareth Cavendish-Smythe, introduced the show. "Welcome, one and all, to the final round of the fourth series of Bletchley Park Challenge. Today, our two finalists, Leeds University and Manchester University, compete head-to-head to see who will crack the codes of our devilish conundrums. The Battle of the North begins!

"Our first team comes from Leeds University and has an average age of twenty-three. They won their three prior engagements with an average score sixty-five points greater than their competitors. The team captain is Poppy Dawson. Leeds University, please introduce yourself."

One by one, the spotlight highlighted the four Leeds contestants as they stated their names and interests. When the last one finished, Cavendish-Smythe moved on to the next team, "Our second team comes from the University of Manchester and has an average age of twenty-four. They're entering the arena with a whopping average score eighty-five points greater than their previous competitors. The team captain is Asher Leek. Manchester University, please introduce yourself."

The spotlight flipped to the other side of the stage, starting with Leek. He stumbled a bit toward the end of his introduction, but Wood artfully picked up the baton and introduced herself next. Were she the petty type, she would have taken pleasure from his fumble, but everyone got a touch of nerves from time to time. By the time Wallace had finished and the APPLAUSE light came on, everyone had already moved on, including the quizmaster.

"We begin with English history; each answer is a date. The answers of the next five questions are related to each other, and together pose our first conundrum. For ten points each, answer the following questions," Cavendish-Smythe started the game. "In what year did the War of 1812 end?"

Leek buzzed in first and Cavendish-Smythe called upon him, "Manchester University, Leek."

"1815," he declared firmly.

"That is correct," Cavendish-Smythe affirmed and rolled into the next question. "In what year was General George Wade authorized by George I to form the six watch companies known as the Black Watch?" Poppy Dawson beat Leek to the buzzer by a split second. "Leeds University, Dawson."

"1881," she answered.

"Incorrect. Minus five points to Leeds. Manchester, your question," Cavendish-Smythe ruled.

Leek buzzed in, sweating under the hot lights but undaunted

by the question. "1725."

"Correct. In what year did William the Conqueror call the Oath of Salisbury?" Cavendish-Smythe read from the card in his hand. He waited for an answer, but none risked a guess, so he answered for them, "1086. William the Conqueror required all landowning men of any account to swear allegiance to be faithful to him in times of crisis.

"Next question: In what year was the Royal Naval Air Service, later called the—"

Leek took a gamble and cut him short with his buzzer and blurted out, "1914." Cavendish-Smythe turned his eyes upward and regarded the interrupter. His stark and chiseled features gave him a strict and austere bearing, temporarily making Leek feel like a child in secondary school about to be scolded by the headmaster.

"Correct," Cavendish-Smythe stated, and took the liberty of prefacing the next question. "Final question before the first conundrum. What year will be the thousandth anniversary of the year in which William the Conqueror commissioned the Domesday Book?"

Leek slammed on his buzzer first again, "2086."

"Incorrect." Cavendish-Smythe's statement didn't parse for Leek at first. He never got a history question wrong. "Minus five points to Manchester. Leeds, an answer?"

All of Dawson's teammates turned their eyes on her; she was the best at history among them. She hazarded a guess, since they would not lose points for a wrong answer under the circumstances. "2085?"

"Correct. The Domesday Book was completed in 1086, but it was commissioned in 1085. The first round ends with Manchester in the lead with twenty-five points. Leeds has five." The quizmaster paused and checked his cards again.

"The answers to the last five questions were 1815, 1725, 1086, 1914, and 2085." As he spoke, the numbers came up on the screen behind him. "As winner of this round, Manchester gets first crack at solving the conundrum. You now have thirty second to find the connection between the five answers." The countdown music started and both teams glommed onto the list of dates. Conundrums were the one time they were allowed to confer amongst themselves instead of answering on their own merits.

In the audience, DCI Jones leaned over to his wife and murmured in a low tone that was barely audible, "It's maths, not dates," he predicted. Sarah nodded but said nothing in reply. He liked to throw out answers at home and she caught his lips moving silently as he processed. She had no doubt that he was keeping a mental count of how many questions he got right and she'd find out how well he did after the show. His all-time best was thirteen questions and three conundrums.

Ten seconds before the music stopped, Dylan Wood of Manchester rang in. "The sum of the numerals in each of the dates equals fifteen."

The lights danced and the music of a conundrum successfully solved swelled and quickly decrescendoed. "That's correct, Wood," Cavendish-Smythe replied once the music was completely silent. "Twenty-five points to Manchester University."

Spirits ran high through the Manchester team. With the first-round jitters gone, both teams buckled in for the next round. Questions and answers volleyed back and forth across the stage, accented by lighting, music, and—for the home viewer—dynamic cuts to different camera angles. Leeds won the following two rounds, but failed to solve the conundrums, leaving them wide open for Manchester, who quickly snatched them up and were ahead by ten despite their overall performance. However, Leeds continued to dominate in the following round as well as crack the fourth conundrum, putting them thirty points ahead of Manchester.

As the show progressed, Leek started to worry. It seemed like everything was unraveling. His sweating had only gotten worse, and he'd started involuntarily rolling his left hand back and forth, like he was conducting or waving a wand. The viewers at home and most of the studio audience were unaware of such developments, as their gaze was drawn to Leeds's runaway streak, but DCI Jones noticed and he was no longer paying attention to the questions or how many he'd gotten right. *There's something wrong with that boy.*

Black covered his microphone as Leeds answered the fifth

round's conundrum and checked in with Leek. "You okay?" he whispered. He'd seen Leek struggle under pressure before, but never like this.

Leek wildly rolled his eyes and responded with a loud, "I am the Walrus. Kookookachoo!" He looked as surprised as his teammates at his own words, which only agitated him more. Cavendish-Smythe turned his attention from the Leeds University team while the audience began to murmur. The lanky blond abruptly stood up and knocked over his seat behind him. The chair crashed onto the floor, stunning the entire studio into silence.

"Don't worry about a thing," he pleaded, swaying in place and barely maintaining his footing. "Every little thing, gonna be all right," he croaked. There was desperation in his voice that contradicted the breezy lyrics. Then, like his chair before him, Asher Leek fell to the floor. The camera and audience lost sight of him as he crumpled behind the Manchester University podium and the studio roared to life. Cavendish-Smythe called for assistance from the studio's first aid director and ordered the crowd to remain in their seats. Leek's teammates, who had front-row seats to his erratic and violent jerking, jumped out of theirs to rush to his aid.

"He's having a seizure!" Black cried out as he kicked Leek's chair out of the way. His younger brother had lived with epilepsy his whole life, and in a surge of adrenaline, Black muscled the shaking quizzer onto his side. "Someone call 999 and start timing this. They'll need to know how long it lasts," he ordered as he put his left arm under Leek's blond head to stop him slamming it against the floor.

The rest of the Manchester team was at a loss of what to do. None of them had their phones with them; all their personal possessions were sitting in lockers in the green room and none of them wore watches—watches were for old people. Cavendish-Smythe kept his cool, however, and noted the time, writing it down on one of his spent question cards. The first aid director arrived within thirty seconds and assessed the situation. With the scene secure, she dialed for emergency services before joining Black at Leek's side.

"He's epileptic?! It wasn't on the release forms," she blurted out to his teammates.

"As far as I know, he's not," Black answered and looked at the other two, Wallace and Woods, who shook their heads in the negative. "At least, he's never mentioned it or had an episode around us before."

Once emergency services answered the call, the first aid director spent the next half minute arranging for an EMS pickup and ordered a stagehand to clear a path and wait for the ambulance at the entrance. The stage director pulled the plug on the live feed and sound and the "on-air" light went dark, but everything was still on and cameras were still recording, although they were no longer broadcasting.

"Ladies and gentlemen, if you would remain calm,

emergency services are on their way!" Cavendish–Smythe projected his voice loudly over the din. He walked next to the Manchester team's podium, eyes on the time—two minutes, fifteen seconds. "How long does one of these last?" he asked Black.

"Anything under five minutes is fine, but doctors start worrying after that," Black said from experience. He'd spent many hours in hospital waiting rooms with his parents. The wait was tense, but there was little anyone could do beyond keeping the young man safe through the episode.

Suddenly Leek stiffened and shouted out loud, and it took Cavendish–Smythe a second to recognize that it was in another language—something like Hindi, or one of the other languages of the subcontinent. As the flood of syllables rolled out, the sentence ended with a scream. Then, all was quiet.

Leek's body went slack and stopped breathing. The first aid director immediately checked for a pulse and started CPR. She called for the AED, but to no avail. By the time EMS arrived, Leek was dead.

Chapter Two

Detroit, Michigan, USA
2nd of December, 7:11 a.m. (GMT-5)

David Emrys Wilson woke to a voice in his head. *I long for the fish from the metal circle and will not wait any longer.* Wilson didn't have to open his eyes to know the speaker, but he did anyway. The silky black cat perched on his chest sat on her haunches, her stance sure and regal. The flashing green of her eyes demanded instant compliance.

"Okay, okay," he said groggily as she stepped off his torso and onto the satiny sheets of his bed. "And it's called tuna, Mau."

She gave him a quizzical look and spoke aloud, "It is not from the metal circle?" The cat's voice was raspy but clear.

"It is," he conceded as he donned a plush robe and slipped his feet into a pair of pink bunny slippers. "But we just call it tuna." The Egyptian Mau flicked her tail indifferently. She preferred it her way; fish did not live in cans.

Mau trailed close behind Wilson as he padded into the kitchen. Her mouth salivated as soon as the pungent smell escaped the tin, but she waited for him to drop the contents of the can—oil and all—into her bowl. It's what normal cats did; she did her best to fit in when it suited her. When she'd first arrived, she'd rip into anything that struck her fancy and ate it, which wasn't so bad with crackers but was a nightmare with cans of tuna. Wilson had negotiated an alternate solution: for food already inside the house, just ask him to retrieve it for her. He suspected he'd only succeeded because she enjoyed being served like royalty.

Wilson placed the bowl on the floor beside the table, and Mau sauntered to the dish, allowing him to scratch behind her ears before she dined. Wilson obliged, and as she devoured her breakfast, he made himself two espressos—the first to be sipped while he read the news of the day, and the second reserved for arts and culture. It had been a little over a month since his return from Avalon, and while he was on leave, he enjoyed a more leisurely pace to adjust to his new circumstances, not least of which was Mau.

Mau was the greatest of cats: the cat that could walk through walls. There were no security measures on the planet—magical or otherwise—that could keep her out. She'd spent the last five thousand years as the mummified pet of the ancient Egyptian priest Hor-Nebwy, a legend in his own right. When Hor-Nebwy summoned her soul from the land of the dead and bound her to him, she was little more than an extension of the mummy priest's will, sent to retrieve things for her master at his behest.

That was how Mau and Wilson had met: a bargain struck to free Wilson from Avalon using Mau's powers. She'd carried him out like a mother cat carrying a kitten. She preferred to carry things in her mouth to maintain her agility and simply grew to accommodate the size of whatever cargo she had. Wilson had personally seen her shift from the size of a housecat to something larger than a tiger to carry him, but he had no idea just how big Mau could grow.

Neither of them could have anticipated what had happened next—in the process of rescuing Wilson from Avalon, he had inadvertently liberated Mau from her servitude. While grooming him, Mau had swallowed a piece of his soul, which had freed her from Hor-Nebwy's esoteric bonds. Mau found she could come and go as she pleased, and she had chosen to stay with Wilson in Detroit. Wilson was flattered, but also a bit exasperated by that choice.

Anyone who has ever tried to train a cat could appreciate Wilson's situation. Even though Mau hadn't been a living cat in the traditional sense for millennia, she was still quintessentially feline. She rankled at the thought of being owned or ordered, and Wilson could understand, given her history. As a matter of course, he refrained from asking her to get him anything, and when he did, it wasn't a request either of them took lightly. His goals and interests were not hers, but they shared a bond and he kept her supplied with tuna.

Wilson took a seat at the kitchen table with his tablet and

started reading the news of the day with his bitter brew. He'd spent enough time as a covert operative—first in the CIA and then in the Salt Mine—to read between the lines, but one need not be a spy to interpret the news as simply a long list of calmly-described horrors. Once Mau finished her food, she licked her paws and cleaned her face as she observed Crawling Shadow—her name for Wilson. Mau saw much through her piercing, pale green eyes.

After she had finished grooming, she jumped onto the table right beside his screen. "I am going to Egypt today," she announced.

Wilson looked up from the screen. "Thank you for telling me. I appreciate it." Mau deigned to acknowledge his praise with the slightest of nods. He'd been working with the magical cat for the past month, trying to acclimatize her to the modern world. It meant acting like a normal cat around most people and instructing her on how to politely interact with the few people that knew who she really was—namely himself, Martinez, Haddock, Hobgoblin, all the people with access to the Salt Mine's sixth floor, and the ghosts of the Quaker family that resided in his Corktown rental home. "When do you think you'll return?" he inquired neutrally and returned to his tablet and another tragedy sanitized by distance and indifference.

It was a ridiculous question, but Crawling Shadow cared for her so Mau answered. "When it is time to return."

"Do you want me to leave food out or will you go hunting?"

He dug for more information in the guise of concern for her appetite.

"I'll hunt," she replied. "I heard a human mention something called a porcupine. I am interested in how it tastes."

The corners of Wilson's mouth twitched but did not break into a grin. "Be careful with that one; it has quills all over it. I wouldn't think it suitable for a meal."

Mau said nothing; she would determine what was to be a meal and what wasn't. She jumped off the table and disappeared at the apex of the leap. It was a regular affair, but it still shook him a little. He was in his very own fortress of solitude: his beloved 500. It was nigh impregnable to small arms and magically warded like crazy, yet Mau came and went as she pleased, as if there was nothing in her way.

He finished the news in peace and moved on to reviews of recent history non-fiction releases. Then he perused cultural events and toyed with the idea of buying a seat to the Detroit Symphony's upcoming performance of Beethoven's Third. It was a month away and he hesitated out of habit. In his profession, he never knew when he would get called to work, and making plans too far into the future seemed a pointless endeavor when he could be whisked away to any place in the world at the drop of a hat.

Over the years, he'd simply stopped making commitments, and it slowly permeated every aspect of his existence. He'd lived a last-minute life in more ways than one. It had never bothered him before, but things were different after his stint in Avalon. Wilson put a reminder in his calendar to see if there were any seats available when the day arrived.

He shut down his tablet and tipped the last drops of his second espresso into his mouth before cleaning the cups and setting them up for tomorrow morning. Wilson had always appreciated order, so much so that he'd tried to reestablish his daily routine. It didn't take long for him to comprehend that a return to the status quo was not possible.

The first clue was that the sound of the Postal Service leaving the distribution center no longer roused him from his sleep. Then, he couldn't muster the will to start his day with calisthenics, as he had done for years. He had always been a small man, just short of five and a half feet, but the muscle mass he'd once taken great pains to cultivate was burned away during his absence. He may have only been gone from the mortal realm for a little over a month, but time passed differently in Avalon. Now, at a whopping 115 pounds, Wilson was medically underweight but he had no interest in force-eating protein and lifting weights. He didn't even crave steak, one of the few things he cooked well and on a regular basis in the past. What had been crucial to his sense of strength and physical prowess was now immaterial.

Wilson tossed through his drawers to find the new clothes that actually fit him; most everything was sized for a version of him that was 150 pounds of lean muscle. Once it became apparent that he was no longer going back to that body, he'd sent all his suits to a local tailor for aggressive alternations and forced himself to buy off-the-shelf casual wear. They were still baggy on him, but he adamantly refused to shop in the boy's department, even if the fit would have been better.

He appraised himself in front of the mirror as he changed for the gym. Touches of gray were just starting to pepper his short dark hair, and all the scars he'd collected over the decades were gone, including the gnarled skin that once passed for a bear mauling. He supposed he should thank Baba Yaga for that unexpected perk to making his soul whole again, but he *did* technically die in the process, so any withheld gratitude seemed reasonable.

He made his way down the spiral staircase into his garage and slid into his British racing green 911. The leather seats were cold against him despite the layers of clothing, and he felt the hum of its engine warming up while he waited for the solid steel jaws of his massive garage door to lift. It was the only way in or out of the 500, at least for anyone that wasn't a cat who could walk through walls. He coaxed the car out into the cold, and after the garage door was completely shut once more, he eased it onto the road.

Wilson had recently changed gyms from one that focused on boxing and lifting to one that had an interior track. His newfound interest in running was perhaps one of the more boggling post-Avalon developments. He had never been one of those people who got a runner's high, and the idea of running in place or in a circuit had seemed futile and counterproductive to the old Wilson. Now, it was almost meditative, a word that wasn't frequently used in his pre-Avalon vocabulary. It didn't hurt that the new gym had a secured and covered parking garage. He loved his Porsche; not even Avalon could change that.

He parked and took the elevator up. As he ascended, he looked out over the Skillman Detroit Public Library and the little patch of greenery that stubbornly refused to yield to the cold. It made him long for spring, when the weather would be more amiable and he could run through West Riverfront Park, not far from the 500. Detroit bloomed in late spring and really was quite beautiful all through summer. Running along the river in the sunshine was going to be fun.

When Wilson made it to the top floor, he queued up his playlist, put it on shuffle, and took off around the track that circled above the rest of the gym. It took a few minutes to warm up, but once he'd lapped the track a few times—each circuit was one-eighth of a mile—he found his stride.

There was no agenda to his running. He didn't keep track of his distance or pace, nor did he worry about improving from his prior day's run. He paid no mind to how many times he passed other runners or the power walkers with their clickers in hand. He just ran, and the simple pleasure of movement took over. He felt like a kid, when the ability to run was a joy in and of itself.

As he slaked his thirst at the water fountain, his stomach forcefully rumbled. It was loud enough that he could actually hear it over the music streaming in through his earpiece, not just feel it. Like a switch being turned off, his desire to run ceased once his body had a new imperative: food. He walked in the slow lane for two laps and toweled off the light sheen of sweat before returning to his car.

The time display lit up after the engine purred to life. *It's almost 11:00?* he thought quizzically. Today was the first day he'd really allowed himself to zone out and run until he got bored of it, and somehow, he'd run for almost three hours without noticing. He did a quick physical assessment and didn't even feel particularly winded or tired, just hungry. It made sense to him that he'd felt okay after his previous shorter runs—after all, he was being careful and easing his way into a new sport—but this was something altogether different.

"Another one for the list," he said aloud to the empty car as he pulled out his phone. His thumbs accessed the encrypted file where he had been keeping track of the post-Baba Yaga-slash-Avalon changes. He could safely ascribe his intact soul and the removal of his scars to the Russian forest witch. He was pretty sure his ability to mentally communicate with Mau—even though he preferred to speak to her out loud whenever possible—was because she had eaten a little piece of his soul in her attempt to heal him in his tattered, shadowy state.

But he was less certain of the cause of the other things, especially the behavioral ones. Did he have his own atheist version of a come-to-Jesus moment? Was it perspective gained through a near-death experience? Was it a newfound appreciation of his intact soul? Would it revert with the passage of time, and he would soon find himself adding protein powder to everything once again? He didn't know the whys and wherefores, only that he was to keep track of them, for himself and the Salt Mine. As far as he knew, he was the only living person who had been to Avalon, and Leader, Chloe, and Dot were extremely interested in the aftereffects.

He scrolled down the list, past "lack of euphoria when casting" followed by a list of spells, rituals, and magical disciplines. Once upon a time, Wilson was one of those magicians that got a rush from casting, and he'd long adjusted his practice to avoid distraction and temptation while he was working. That was, in part, how he became a master summoner; it was one of the few arcane disciplines that didn't get him as high as a kite. It's what made the Magh Meall extra special to Wilson in the past: it was one of the few places where he could cast freely without feeling doped up. But now there was no spell that elicited such a response, and he had tried them all. Wilson was ever dogged and thorough when it came to flushing out the unseen.

Once he got to the bottom of the list, he tapped out "Can run for a long time" and hit save. It didn't sound like much, but it was an undeniable physical change, and all changes went on the list. Output was only as good as the input, and he always tried to be honest with processing data.

When he got back to the 500, he took a quick shower and tried to beat the lunch rush at his local Greek place. He was itching for a falafel salad with extra bread and an overabundance of tzatziki sauce. He dug into his meal, savoring every crispy, spicy bite and creamy slather until he reached the end. That was another change he noted: food tasted better. The old Wilson fundamentally regarded food as fuel, and things tasted nicer when they had more calories. In the course of having his soul torn asunder, dying, awakening in Avalon, burning said soul to escape the rolling green hills, and returning to the mortal realm by legendary cat, he had acquired a palate.

He was considering a piece of baklava and a Turkish coffee when his phone rang. The sound of the specialized ringtone took him by surprise; it had been ages since he'd gotten a call from the Salt Mine.

"Hello," he answered.

"Fulcrum, you've been activated," David LaSalle's crisp voice came through the line. "Please come to the Mine. There's a mission waiting."

Chapter Three

Detroit, Michigan, USA
2nd of December, 2:15 p.m. (GMT-5)

"How've you been, Mr. Watson? Haven't seen you in a while," the gregarious gate guard greeted Wilson as he stepped out of his station.

"I've been taking some time off, but all good things must come to an end." Wilson made conversation as he presented the Discretion Minerals ID that identified him as Davis Watson, Director of Acquisitions. "You working the second shift now, George?"

The guard looked up from the ID badge and visually verified it was Mr. Watson. The car and the face were the same as before, but George would have bet dollars to donuts that this was the first time he'd addressed him by his name. "Naw, just pulling a double today. Got to save up for holidays," he explained. "It's the twins' first Christmas and the wife's gone a little overboard, not that the little ones care—they'd be just as happy playing with the wrapping paper and boxes."

Wilson nodded sympathetically as George handed him back his ID, "Hard to say no when it's for the kids at Christmas time."

"No matter how much she spends, it's still cheaper than a divorce." George winked conspiratorially as he waved Wilson through the raised gate. "You take care. Those minerals aren't going to acquire themselves," he joked.

Wilson smirked. "Indeed." He pulled through the gate and entered Zug Island, home to Discretion Minerals. The company started out over a hundred years ago mining the vast salt deposits underground, and was bought by the CIA in the 50s as part of the MKULTRA project. Since the purchase, it had expanded its operations from mining salt under Detroit to providing a plausible cover for the Salt Mine, the black ops organization tasked with keeping magical activity in check. Every country in the world had natural resources, and mineral scouting justified their agents' presence worldwide. Governments and leaders came and went, but as a general rule, no one wanted to refuse a potential injection of American dollars into their wallets.

Wilson backed into his old parking space and habit took over as he approached the elevators and flipped out the special titanium key that allowed the carriage to descend into the Salt Mine instead of going up into Discretion Minerals HQ. When the doors finally opened, he stepped into the barren metal room and caught sight of Angela Abrams, the attendant that prevented anything dangerous from entering or leaving the Mine. She was blonde now, and Wilson had never noticed how pretty she was before, even as the thick ballistic glass between them distorted her likeness ever so slightly.

Abrams looked up from her magazine and squealed at the sight of him. "Wilson!" sounded through the crackly old speaker system. He was still painfully thin, but the cut of his expertly tailored suit hung well on his frame. Only those who had known him previously would have felt his thinness out of place. "You'll have to tell me where you've been. Most people come back from vacation tanned and fat."

"Angela, you're a picture and don't let anyone tell you otherwise," he stated emphatically as he placed his Glock 26 and Korchmar Monroe attaché into the slot for security. "I heard I missed all sorts of excitement while I was away…" he opened the door for her to share gossip—if she was filling him in, she wasn't asking him questions.

"Mr. Wilson, you know I can't discuss such things. I am the soul of discretion," she answered coquettishly as the mechanical noises whirled away. "But I can tell you about my latest trip to Niagara with my new fella."

"The Canadian side, I hope," Wilson played along.

"Of course," she sardonically replied. "We got on the water in one of the boat tours and afterward had a rack of lamb to die for at a restaurant overlooking the falls."

The beep of the scanners cut short her account, indicating that Wilson and his possessions were good to enter the Mine. Abrams buzzed him through, and as he collected his belongings, her voice came over the speaker on the other side of the sigiled threshold. "Welcome back, Wilson."

He smiled and nodded before walking down the long metal corridor to the pair of elevators. Taking the one on the left, he presented his palm and retina—standard operating procedure if you wanted it to actually move. Once he had the green light, he pressed the button for the fourth floor and went deeper into the complex. Normally, he would have first made a stop at his office on the fifth floor, but Leader was expecting him and it wasn't wise to keep her waiting.

The elevator doors opened to a foyer manned by David LaSalle, Leader's private secretary-slash-bodyguard. No one got to Leader without going through him first. His administrative skills were impeccable; he kept methodical files, could type eighty words a minute, and make arrangements for the movement of people and goods anywhere in the world at the drop of a hat. He was also a brick of a man at six-foot-three and 230 pounds, with the esoteric and martial skills required for his unique position.

The two men acknowledged each other with a curt nod, which sufficed as a greeting between the two professionals. Wilson took a seat in the one of the chairs along the wall while LaSalle informed Leader of his arrival. Wilson could hear a rumble of a response, but he couldn't make out the exact words from here. LaSalle curtly nodded despite the fact that Leader wasn't in the room to see the gesture. "Of course, ma'am."

LaSalle secured his work and rose, towering over Wilson.

"Leader's ready for you." He motioned for Wilson to follow. "You're still looking thin. Didn't Martinez send half the leftovers home with you?" There was a familiarity in his tone that Wilson was unaccustomed to. He'd never known LaSalle to be a particularly chatty or emotive person in all their years of interaction, but all that changed over Thanksgiving when LaSalle, wearing a sweater and jeans instead of a suit, crossed over the Corktown house's threshold carrying homemade sweet potato pies. During the course of the evening, he'd exhibited spontaneous facial expressions, laughed out loud, and engaged in light conversation. Perhaps most discombobulating for Wilson, LaSalle had been without Leader.

Wilson grinned. "You forget, I have a cat now. She can really pack it in." LaSalle almost smiled.

Both men instinctually straightened up as they approached Leader's office. LaSalle knocked before announcing, "Fulcrum to see you, ma'am."

"Show him in," the firm mid-range voice ordered from the other side. Wilson straightened his suit by the cuffs as LaSalle opened the door.

The room hadn't changed since the last time Wilson had been inside. Cut out of the salt itself, the walls gleamed crystalline white with flecks and streaks of impurities. It was twice the size of an agent's office, and most of the space was dedicated to a row of filing cabinets behind Leader's large and utilitarian desk. The only ornamentation on the walls was an excellent reproduction of *The Temptation of Saint Anthony* by Jan Brueghel the Elder. The chairs were still overly wide and lower than Leader's chair, and Wilson took a seat at her instigation as she put away a file, only to retrieve a set of different files.

Wilson heard the door close behind him as LaSalle took his leave. The familiar butterflies fluttered in his stomach, but his impassive face betrayed nothing—visiting Leader was always an event. She was a petite woman—slim and just shy of five feet tall—with salt and pepper hair and a wardrobe that favored practical over executive. While she superficially resembled a Vermont maple syrup farmer who knitted her own sweaters and composted, her piercing gray eyes and unrelenting will dispossessed anyone of such a comparison. There was nothing frivolous or unintentional about her. She was chiseled from granite, and in the world of chaos, she was constant—a Gibraltar in the clandestine world of theirs.

"Nice to have you back, Fulcrum," she greeted him.

"Nice to be back," he replied honestly.

Pleasantries exchanged, Leader passed over a stack of files. "Over the past six months, there have been three unexplained deaths in the United Kingdom. All of the deceased were university students. The most recent victim was Asher Leek."

Wilson tiled his head and raised a single brow. "Of the Yorkshire Leeks?" They were one of the oldest—and *the* wealthiest—magical families in England.

"The very same," Leader confirmed.

Wilson opened the top file and flipped until he found a picture of the lanky young man with a mop of blond hair. "It says he died the 4th of last month. Why the delay?"

"The family initially wanted to handle it themselves. They have since exhausted their resources and came up short," Leader said with just a hint of schadenfreude. *Par for the course,* Wilson thought to himself. He shared her disdain of how they handled esoteric matters across the pond.

When the Mine came into existence in the 1950s, it had pushed hard for the United Kingdom to create a fellow organization to help combat the influence of the CCCP's Ivory Tower. The old magic families of the UK had strongly resisted a formal agency, asserting that they could restrain and control the use of magic themselves as they had for centuries via the Dawn Club. They saw no need to get the government involved, and their influence prevented the creation of a British counterpart to help monitor and control magical threats on the Isle.

The refusal to form their own institution resulted in Salt Mine agents visiting the UK whenever there was an esoteric mess, especially in more recent years. Wilson alone had racked up a ton of airline miles across all his aliases, thanks to the lack of initiative of the Dawn Club. What the old guard couldn't foresee—or simply refused to accept—was the massive social change to Anglo-American culture in modern times. After two world wars, the masses weren't interested in returning to the old ways, where "polite society" meant "obey what your betters say." The pull of the old families grew weaker each year, which only made them more recalcitrant and certain that their way was best.

"Oh, how the mighty have fallen," Wilson snidely remarked.

Leader ignored his moment of frankness and continued with the briefing. "They've reached out to us and have asked us to investigate due to the suspicious circumstances of his death."

"Suspicious?" he queried as he closed the file and directed his full attention to Leader. She didn't call him here to watch him read, and there would be plenty of time to review the contents during travel.

"Young Mr. Leek had a seizure and died immediately. Upon autopsy, there was significant atrophy of the frontal cortex and numerous amyloid plaques," she responded.

Wilson leaned forward in his seat. "Twenty-one is a little young for early-onset Alzheimer's."

"Exactly. It was doubly dubious considering he had no history of neurologic problems. Luckily, Mr. Leek died on camera while filming a quiz show." Leader swiveled her monitor around and played the Bletchley Park Challenge footage. She had already seen it numerous times and watched Wilson in her peripheral vision instead.

"What that he's saying at the end?" Wilson inquired. "It is Hindi?"

"Close. It's Sanskrit, a language Mr. Leek had not studied," Leader highlighted the incongruity. "Chloe identified it as an excerpt from the third brahmanam of the fourth chapter of the *Brihadaranyaka Upanishad.* The full passage and a translation is included in the file."

Wilson nodded. As far as he was concerned, the conjoined twins that served as the Mine's librarians were the final word when it came to esoteric knowledge. He got down to brass tacks. "What are my working parameters?"

"Infiltration under the guise of diplomatic assistance," Leader spelled it out as she reoriented her screen. "The Leeks are desperate and have opened up their familial estate to the Mine's representative. Obviously, see if the death of Asher Leek is anything that should concern us, but what we are really after is intel. Gather as much information as you can about Buttercrambe Hall, the Leek family, and anything regarding the standings of the Dawn Club. Don't hesitate to extend your stay by investigating the other deaths as well, for completeness sake."

Wilson read between the lines. "Understood," he answered firmly.

"Good. Stop by the sixth floor for specialized gear—Weber is expecting you. Your flight leaves this evening."

Chapter Four

Detroit, Michigan, USA
2nd of December, 2:50 p.m. (GMT-5)

Harold Weber fiddled with a prototype that was being particularly difficult. The mechanics were right and the magic applied with precision. On paper, it should work, but it didn't. It was in these moments that he was certain inanimate objects had some sort of quiescent will that only arose to test his patience. He stepped back and pulled off his gloves in exasperation. He pushed his safety goggles into his unruly white hair and said some choice words in his native German.

He heard the steps coming down the hall—hard-soled shoes grinding on the saline floor. It wasn't Chloe and Dot; there weren't enough feet and they tended to wear softer soles. His workshop was tucked away in an offshoot of the long hall to the Library on the sixth floor and didn't lend itself to accidental visitors, which left few options for the owner of those steps.

"Fulcrum," Weber greeted Wilson as he entered the workshop.

"Weber," Wilson replied with a slight nod.

"You really hit the jackpot this time," the Mine's

quartermaster commented as he straightened his thick-lens glasses and wiped his hands down on a cleanish rag tucked into one of the numerous pockets of his work apron. There was a twinkle in his blue eyes.

Wilson let one side of his mouth lift up in an almost-smile—leave it to Weber to be business as usual. Not one comment on his absence, ordeal, or thinness. No chit chat about their shared Thanksgiving meal or polite inquiries about his cat. Straight to the gear for the mission; it was refreshing. "What do you have for me today?"

"Perhaps the better question would be what don't I have for you today?" The old man grinned like a kid in a candy store. "The fourth floor has pulled out all the stops for this one."

Weber was a magician of the rarest type: he could make magic work with technology. He was always tinkering with the next creation in search of the perfect mix of elegant design and utility. The former engineer turned Salt Mine inventor had designed all of the agents' specialized gear. Sometimes they were purely magical, but more often than not, they were mundane items to which he'd incorporated magic. He'd been adapting standard CIA gear with arcane uses for decades. As technology advanced, so did Weber, both in skill and age. Even though he was old enough to retire, the thought never occurred to him. He thrived on mental stimulation, and to him, retirement was only going to be a pine box.

He motioned for Wilson to follow him to the back of the

room and presented him with a super-sized version of the Mine's standard issue luggage. Wilson looked it over. If it was like its predecessor, its hard case was a mix of Kevlar and polycarbonate, rendering it equal to 3A body armor. Inside, there would be a collection of listening devices, two nearly unbreakable knives made of carbon fiber and glass, and a concealed compartment large enough for a disassembled firearm or other small illicit items. The entire thing would be covered in a covert lining for the benefit of airport x-rays, detectors, or scans.

"You got me bigger luggage?" Wilson asked sarcastically.

Weber gave him a droll stare. "Take a look inside," he suggested a little too innocently. Wilson complied and was disappointed to find the suitcase empty except for two wooden foot-long rulers crudely taped together, forming a twenty-four-inch-long unit. "Now, close it, set the lock tumblers to 1776, then to 1989, and then to 2001."

Wilson followed his instructions to the letter and as the last tumbler fell into place, the luggage suddenly shrank down to carry-on size with a pop no louder than a crisp snap of the fingers. "Remarkable," he complimented the inventor.

The Cheshire grin on Weber's face told him there was more. "Open it up."

Wilson released the catches, but when he opened the case, it was filled with men's clothing. "Okay, that's cool," he conceded.

Weber clapped his hands with glee. "They're coterminous

extradimensional spaces!" He went to another table in the room and pulled the original suitcase from underneath. He hoisted it on top of that table and opened to show Wilson it was in fact the same container. Wilson felt like he was part of an elaborate magic act, the kind that had and abundance of sequins and no karmic backlash. "Now, go through the sequence again."

They both closed their respective cases, and Wilson rolled the wheel of numbers with his thumbs. He pulled the string of numbers using the mnemonic pictures he'd imprinted the first time Weber had given him the string of combinations: Declaration of Independence, the fall of the Berlin Wall, and the smoking towers of 9/11. The case in front of Wilson grew back to extra-large size, again popping, while Weber's shrank to carry-on.

Wilson immediately glommed onto the tactical uses in the field. Weber had effectively created control teleportation between two discrete containers. Wilson could keep his real gear in the safety of his home but have access to it at the drop of a hat. A wolfish smile emerged. "What's the range?"

"Unlimited!" Weber burst with pride.

"What about wards? Can the cases travel through wards?"

Weber shook his head. "Sadly no. You can form exceptions in your personal wards, but if the place where you are currently located is warded again such magic, it won't work."

Wilson started running different scenarios in his head. "Can I leave one at the Salt Mine for immediate supply runs?"

"No," Weber lamented. "Leader is unwilling to make any exceptions in the Mine's wards. Currently, they are an open two-way communication, meaning the switch can be activated on either unit. Should an agent lose control of their suitcase, it could be used to send something unsavory to its mate, such as a bomb. Or worse."

"Right. Don't lose your luggage. Check," Wilson confirmed.

Weber's face became very serious as he assumed his role as health and safety officer. "Follow standard protocol regarding extradimensional spaces. More specifically, do *not* put the smaller carry-on inside the bigger one. That goes for any other magical items that incorporate extradimensional spaces."

"Even if they're packed in salt or sealed in warded containers?" Wilson asked.

Weber gave him a cautionary look. "Yes. Leave that to the specialists." He waited while the pregnant pause emphasized the importance of this point. He'd long since learned the value of repeating the obvious in as many different ways as possible.

"Okay, no stashing pocket dimensions inside my new luggage," Wilson verbalized his understanding of the rules.

A lightness came over Weber as he proceeded, "There are a number of smaller upgrades as well." He pointed out a line of round, thin lithium batteries next to a black brick about the size of four phones stacked upon each other. "They look like coin cells, even down to the markings on the case, but they're upgraded versions of the standard listening devices in your luggage. I've managed to increase both their range and durability by about ten percent"

Wilson fingered the new piece and couldn't find the depressor to activate it. "No more buttons?"

"No," Weber spoke and took one in hand to show Wilson how to operate it before he broke something. "To activate them, just rotate the two lids like you're unscrewing a jar."

He put down the bug and picked up the black brick next to it. "I've done the same with the transmitter amplifier as well. We should get three to four months of transmission before we run out of power." The Mine's transmitters boosted the bug's signals via encrypted public cell phone frequencies. He passed the block to Wilson, who noted its new rubbery coating. "I've also made it water-resistant." Weber was never one to rest of his laurels.

Wilson looked the device over and noted that the on/off switch was in the same location, only it was now sealed with rubberized gaskets. As soon as he put the amplifier down, Weber handed him a new saltcaster. "This is almost identical to your old saltcaster, but I've slightly increased the storage chamber and reduced the grain size for six uses per cartridge. I've also changed the design to accept replaceable salt packs for faster recharge in the field. There are four additional charges next to the bugs."

The saltcaster, a Weber original invention, was by far and away the most used tool in the field. When he'd found a way to capture residual magical signatures, the Salt Mine had an entire newly method of identifying and tracking magic use and supernatural creatures. The genius behind the device was that it magically enhanced the salt blown out of the runed chamber. Any pattern formed in the dispersed salt was a unique signature that could be catalogued and indexed, resulting in the Mine's extensive database of practitioners, demons, devils, fae, special ghosts, and other creatures. Over the years, there had been many iterations, the recent models disguised as boxy vape pens.

"Additionally, the wifi jammer in the butt now also affects PnP cable transmissions at a range of ten yards. It'll also jam a RG59 coaxial cable, but you have to be within ten feet. After a jam, you should have about ten to twenty seconds of interference to make a move."

"Which is it?" Wilson tried to pin him down on a number. There was a huge difference between ten and twenty seconds in the field.

Weber made an ambivalent face and shrugged his shoulders. "If you want to be conservative, assume you have six seconds and don't try to play the edges. I'd like to be more specific but, there's no way I can give you a better estimate. It all depends on the topography, the thickness of the walls—" Weber's forthcoming digression into physical and electronic shielding was cut short by a boisterous yell.

"You're back!" Chloe exclaimed from the doorway into Weber's workshop.

"Gah! Give me a warning when you're going to do that." Dot recoiled from the high-pitched shrill but there was only so much distance she could get, being joined at the hip to her sister. "You know we literally just saw him four days ago."

"That's Dot-speak for 'glad you see you back in the saddle,'" Chloe translated for her as she leaned in to give Wilson a hug. Dot refrained due to the box cradled in her arms but gave him a nod. "We've got the goods for you this time..." Chloe intoned at a significantly lower volume.

Wilson wasn't an affectionate person as a general rule, but he made an exception for the twins. They had saved his hide more times than he could count, and they had become the little sisters he'd never had—though he was certain they were older than him, even if they didn't show it. Chloe was on the right and Dot on the left—both dirty blonde and gifted with an eidetic memory, but that's where their similarities ended.

"Beware of librarians bearing gifts?" Wilson stage whispered to Weber as he returned the gesture of affection.

"This isn't a gift. It's a loan," Dot said surlily as she placed the box on the table. Wilson and Weber recognized it as a containment box. They came in different sizes, depending on what was stored within, but they were nearly the same in concept: a wooden exterior into which runes and sigils were carved, a thin layer of lead lining on the inside, and packed with salt. Consequently, they were always heavy for their size, and there was a resounding thud as Dot unburdened herself of the package.

"What's in the box?" Wilson asked, knowing full well it was something powerful from deeper in the Mine.

Dot broke the seal with her will, like slicing along a seam of tape with a utility knife. She put her hand into the salt and cradled a smooth circular piece of granite about the size of a half-dollar. The salt spilled back into the box from the hole in the middle. "One hag stone," she said as she placed it on the table. Wilson was well versed with the powers of the item: looking through the hag stone allowed one to see the supernatural. It was like stepping into a sepia photograph: everything that was mundane faded into the monochrome background, while magical things were enhanced.

It was extremely useful, but the Mine didn't let it out much. It was dangerous to look through it for long periods of time as it tended to thin the barrier between realms, allowing creatures to pass over. "No more than ten seconds at a time; no more than three passes at any one location," Chloe reminded him. It wasn't a safe limit—magic was never safe—but it was the threshold where no one would call him an idiot if something did go wrong.

"Yes, Mom," Wilson petulantly replied.

Dot rummaged through the salt and carefully brought up another item: a ring. Wilson made a sour face; he hated magical rings, as so many of them were effectively cursed—they had the fairest of faces yet the blackest of hearts. It was so easy for one to think they were the master of such a small and decorative thing, but magical rings were pernicious and the unobservant wearer could slowly find their will worn away until they were slaves to the magic of the ring. Unfortunately, they tended to be the most powerful of items, and their utility drove their overuse.

This one was made of gold and etched with Futhark runes. It landed heavy on the table as it slid out of Dot's hand. "This is Andvaranaut," she informed them. Both men recoiled at her words despite the twin's ease. Andvaranaut was the ring forged by the *Nibelung* Andvari, the very ring about which Wagner crafted his epic opera *Der Ring des Nibelungen.* It was thoroughly cursed and, in the right—or wrong—hands, immensely powerful.

Wilson was the first to regain his composure and put his hands out in protest. "I'm sure I won't be needing that."

"Don't be a baby; it doesn't bite," Dot taunted him. "All it does is help you find what you want."

"Oh, I'm well aware of what it does, and the last thing I need is to find what I want," Wilson objected. He could think of fewer curses more devastating that giving someone their heart's desire.

"You're taking the ring, Wilson," Chloe cut to the chase. "You don't have to wear it unless you need it, but you're taking it. This may be the only chance we get at the Leeks of Buttercrambe Hall, and we aren't going to waste an opportunity just because you are squeamish about a magic ring. That's what we're trained to do, remember?"

Wilson acquiesced, but insisted that it be put on a chain and in its own secure pouch. He was used to Dot being the blunt one, and if Chloe was putting her foot down, he knew the issue was no longer up for debate. Dot snickered at her sister's brusque diatribe. People always thought of Chloe as the sweet one, but she knew just how sharp her sister's barbs could be. Dot motioned for her sister to retrieve the final item from the box, a reward for laying down the law so aptly.

Chloe graciously accepted her sister's courtesy and pushed her hand into the salt. She sifted the grains through her extended fingers and lifted a rust-red crystal several inches in length. "This is a true Gomeda," she enumerated the final piece of magical kit. The light caught one of its facets, and it sparkled fiercely now that it was free of the salt.

"Wait, how long have we had that?" Weber queried and took it from Chloe's hands. "I'm sure I could have used it for all sorts of things," he objected.

"It's the only one we have," Dot explained. "If we find another, I'm sure Leader would consider letting this one out of the vault for you to play with." Weber was too preoccupied looking for his jeweler's loupe to notice her dig.

Wilson racked his brain but came up blank. "Anyone want to clue me in?"

"It's a hessonite crystal—a type of garnet," Weber spouted

factoids as he examined it under magnification.

"And what's this magical garnet do?" Wilson asked.

"It's one of the true nine gems of the Navaratna. When a little blood is applied to it, it summons the power of Rahu to cloak you in shadow, effectively making you invisible until the blood dries out," Chloe chimed in to Wilson's relief.

"Wait, I'm the top infiltration asset and this is the first I'm hearing about a gem that makes you invisible?" he balked.

"Like a said, we aren't going to waste this unique opportunity," Chloe sidestepped his recrimination.

"I wonder what kind of vision it works on," Weber muttered to him. "The naked eye obviously, but what about magical sight? Or cameras?"

Dot hesitated and looked at Chloe, who shrugged, "We don't know."

Weber looked over his glasses and down his nose. "We would have known if I was given access to it earlier."

Chloe huffed. "Fine. Let's test it now before we send Wilson out in the field with it. You can do the bleeding."

The German perked up and practically kicked his heels on his way to his tools. If he'd heard the terseness in Chloe's voice, he didn't show it. He set up different types of surveillance, including thermal and infrared, and asked the twins to monitor them. He asked Wilson to man the hag stone and prepared to prick himself with his pen needle.

Weber held the tip firm against the lateral side of his fourth finger and pressed the button. The small sharp lancet pricked fast and deep and a bleb of blood welled on his digit. "Here's goes nothing," he said as he smeared the drop on the crystal and disappeared from view. Weber walked back and forth across the workshop, waiting for input.

Wilson held the piece of granite to his eye and looked through the hole. All the magical equipment Weber was working on lit up, but no Weber. "I can't see you through the hag stone," Wilson reported as he pulled it away from his eye.

"We can see you on the cameras," Dot hollered.

"Which ones?" Weber's disembodied voice asked.

"All of them," Chloe answered.

"Interesting," Weber mused, pacing. "It grants invisibility from visual sight—even magically enhanced sight—but not technology." He wiped the residual blood off the stone with a tissue and blinked back into sight. "Stay away from security cameras, Fulcrum," he cautioned Wilson as he put the true Gomeda on the table.

"I didn't need a magical gem to know that," he replied dryly.

Chapter Five

Detroit, Michigan, USA
2nd of December, 7:25 p.m. (GMT-5)

Wilson had arrived at Detroit Metropolitan Airport with an hour to spare before his flight. Packing for the trip was easy enough, but it had taken several hours to form an exception to his wards that would allow them to swap freely while he was away. And then there was the matter of Mau. It felt strange having to tell someone that he needed to travel for work at the last minute. With the exception of living with Alex—Aaron, his name was Aaron now—Wilson had always lived alone.

He wasn't worried about who would take care of Mau; clearly, she could fend for herself. No, he was more concerned about what she would do to his place in his absence. Thankfully, Martinez offered to open cans of tuna in his place; the last thing he needed during a mission was Mau appearing out of thin air demanding food.

With a one-way ticket in hand and his car in long-term parking, Wilson took a seat near his gate and kept his coterminous extradimensional carry-on close by. Detroit Metro Airport was much the same as the last time he'd flown. He was a seasoned traveler and enjoyed the anonymity that came with airports. He was just another guy waiting for his flight and looking at his phone to bide the time. Unbeknownst to all who passed him, he was reading a translation of *Brihadaranyaka Upanishad*, Chapter 4, Brahmanam 3, Hymns 20-22, which discussed the premises of moksha: liberation, freedom, emancipation, and self-realization.

> 4.3.20: Now when (he feels) as if he were being killed or overpowered, or being pursued by an elephant, or falling into a pit, (in short) conjures at the time through ignorance whatever terrible things he has experienced in the waking state, (that is the dream state). And when (he becomes) a god, as it were, or a king, as it were, or thinks, "This (universe) is myself, I am this altogether," that is his highest world.
>
> 4.3.21: This indeed is his (true) form, beyond desires, free from evil, and fearless. As a man, when embraced by a beloved wife, knows nothing that is without, nothing that is within, thus this person, when embraced by the Supreme Self, knows nothing that is without, nothing that is within. This indeed is his (true) form, in which his wishes are fulfilled, in which the Self only is his wish, in which no other wish is left, he is free from any sorrow.
>
> 4.3.22: In this state, a father is no father, a mother

> no mother, the worlds no worlds, the gods no gods, the Vedas no Vedas. In this state a thief is no thief, the killer of a noble Brahmana no killer, a Candala no Candala, a Pulkasa no Pulkasa, a monk no monk, a hermit no hermit. (This form of his) is untouched by good work and untouched by evil work, for he is then beyond all the woes of his heart (intellect).

Heavy shit for a twenty-one-year-old, Wilson thought to himself as he closed the file and reviewed the timeline. The first death had occurred on June 8th. The victim, Paul Youngblood, was a fifteen-year-old in his second year studying physics at the University of Leeds. He was found dead in a study room by a student worker who was making the rounds at the end of the night. According to the security footage, he entered alone, no one joined him, and he'd had a seizure an hour before closing time. The coroner found severe brain atrophy similar to Alzheimer's, but indicated that he'd never seen such in a heretofore-healthy person.

The second death occurred three months later. The victim was Zadie Gourlay, a twenty-year-old third-year student of English Literature at the University of Liverpool. She'd suffered a seizure during soccer practice. She died on the way to the hospital. The autopsy noted a similar deterioration of the brain

Then, there was the untimely demise of Asher Williams Wilson Durand Leek, the eldest son of Marmaduke Williams

Wilson Durand Leek and Vavasour de Klerk Durand Leek. Wilson's eyes glazed over the litany of names, knowing what it meant. Once British families had accumulated a certain amount of wealth, they invariably started collecting names—the more, the better. The emphasis on class was one aspect of British society that rankled Wilson. He cared little about pedigree for prestige sake. To quote the immortal Joe Strummer, "*I don't wanna hear about what the rich are doing, I don't wanna go to where the rich are going*." Give him the family tree of a devil or a fae any day—knowing *that* bloodline had real value.

Unfortunately, the Leeks were an old magical family, and he had to know all the gnarled branches of that family tree for the mission, so he dove in. The Leeks first appeared in the UK in the late ninth century, arriving on English soil as Viking leaders in the Great Heathen Army. They eventually settled in Yorkshire, but acquired several large family estates throughout all of England via marriage. They were hugely influential in British society in the sixteenth to nineteenth centuries, when son after son either entered the navy, invested in technology such as coal and rail, or traveled to India where they diligently siphoned the wealth of the subcontinent to England's verdant shores via their coffers. In modern times, they'd avoided making anything of use to the world and instead focused solely on financial investments.

Wilson skimmed over swaths of Leek family history and cherry-picked the sprawling genogram for the twelve members of the family he was likely to encounter at Buttercrambe Hall. The familial estate was home to members of three distinct branches: the Durand Leeks, the Vries Leeks, and the FitzAlan Leeks.

The matriarch of the family was Cordelia Rosamund Camise Durand Leek, Countess of Stamford. The sixty-nine-year-old woman hadn't left the estate in more than a decade, preferring to call the shots from her favorite parlor chair. Her closest confidant was her late husband's spinster sister, Imogen Alexandra Nina Durand Leek, age sixty-seven, who had lived her whole life at Buttercrambe. Cordelia had one son and three daughters, but the only one living at Buttercrambe was her son Marmaduke Williams Wilson Durand Leek, age forty-six, with his wife Vavasour de Klerk Durand Leek, age forty, and their two remaining children: Ferris Arthur Thomas Durand Leek, age nineteen, and Millicent Alice Tuppence Durand Leek, age sixteen. The last Durand Leek at Buttercrambe was Arthur Williams Walter Durand Leek, age forty-five, the last surviving child of Cordelia's dead brother-in-law William.

The rest of the Leeks living at Buttercrambe were from the other two branches: three Vries Leeks and two FitzAlan Leeks. Basil Grant Thomas Vries Leek, age thirty-five, and his younger sister Bellasis Vyner Vries Leek, age thirty, were frequent visitors to Buttercrambe Hall in their youth, favored by their Aunt Imogene, who was godmother to them both. They eventually came to live there as they fell out of favor with their own parents; in Bellasis's case, she came with her illegitimate daughter, Roos Adriana Maria Vries Leek, age sixteen. Roos's father was a mystery for some time and now was only derogatorily referred to as "The Dutchman" by the rest of the family. The final two residents were Grant Henry Roger FitzAlan Leek, age fifty-two, and his sister Curwen Elizabeth FitzAlan Leek, age fifty. They were devoted to each other and never married. There was talk of branches of the family tree crossing, but as far as anyone knew, none had borne fruit.

Wilson closed the file, his mind swimming with eleventy-one names between the twelve of them. There was more information to read—the staff, their financials, and the various corporate shelters they used to safeguard their wealth—but he put it aside for the flight. It was a direct overnight, and he could use it to lull himself to sleep for a few hours of shuteye. He turned his attention on something more concrete: Buttercrambe Hall itself.

Buttercrambe Hall was a large Gothic Revival, built around the remains of the earlier house that mostly succumbed to fire in 1786. Wilson zoomed in on the pictures of the exterior—to call it a country house was an understatement, if technically true. A more appropriate term would be a great house or a power house: one of the English palaces built to display the owner's power and wealth. The edifice sprawled beyond a hundred yards in width and its lofty three stories towered over the manicured greens. It had one hundred seventy-five rooms, forty staff bedrooms, ten offices, twenty bathrooms, and four large staterooms on three hundred acres of garden, forest, and field. There was an indoor pool and two libraries, one in which they'd *found* a First Folio of Shakespeare five years ago.

Wilson tried to image a place where such a thing was lying around, waiting to be rediscovered, but failed to fathom such opulence. Where every piece of furniture was custom built for the space, the decor was priceless works of art, and exquisite tapestries—the largest collection second only to the Royal collection— graced the walls. The Hall was built around the Grand Chamber, the lone surviving chamber of the original house and an exceptional example of late Elizabethan interior design. It was sixty feet square and wainscoted in oak, darkened by age and intricately carved and painted. The paneling alone was insured for half a million pounds. Above the wainscoting was a long frieze of baronial arms related to Yorkshire that stretched back to the late thirteenth century.

Wilson looked up from his phone at the masses of people mulling near the gate and the uptick of activity around the counter. He got his things ready for boarding and thought about how he wanted to play his hand. He often approached the upper crust of society with the concern and deference they had grown accustomed to. Coming in as the hired help—albeit in the six-figure range—made it easier for him to manipulate them into doing what he wanted them to do.

However, this situation was different. The Leeks had asked

for help and they would know he was a representative of the Salt Mine. Perhaps it was time for a little friction that would reveal more about the old family—like a steel brush against rusty iron instead of his normal sensitive polish to the tea silver. He could play with type: the brash American that didn't play by the rules but was to be tolerated because he was useful. The thought tempted him; it would certainly be more fun than pretending to be the toady. After all, they were one of the ones who'd deemed the Salt Mine unnecessary—that is, until *they* needed them.

Chapter Six

Baraga, Michigan, USA
20th of November, 1:00 p.m. (GMT-5)

Cordelia rose from the lounge chair and made another pass to the window. The weather had turned decidedly gloomy, and she looked for signs of their impending visitor through the fat raindrops. She held herself proudly, and her tall thin frame cut a stark figure against the dim light eking out through the storm clouds. It was her fourth such circuit in the past hour, and a huff escaped her.

"When is that dratted man going to be here?" she addressed her sister-in-law over her shoulder. Cordelia was not known for many virtues, and patience wasn't even on the list.

Imogene hid her smirk behind her book—the copy of *Little Women* she'd received on her twelfth birthday so many years ago. The tome bore the scars of being well read and well loved, before Imogene had learned to take care of precious things instead of taking them for granted. She made a habit of rereading the title every December. The words hadn't changed, but as time passed, their meanings did. When she was younger, she'd closely associated herself with Jo, but now, it was Beth who was nearest to her heart.

"It's miserable out there. I wouldn't be surprised if he's stuck in traffic or there was a delay at the airport." she replied without looking up from her reading.

Cordelia sighed heavily as Imogene turned the page. "This wouldn't have happened if they had allowed us to arrange travel," she asserted.

Imogene could no longer hold her tongue. She slid a bookmark into place and set the book down on her lap. "You're the one who invited them into our business," she reminded her sister-in-law. There was a nobility in her delicate features, a softness than cushioned the harsh truth of her words. She was a stark beauty in her youth, but she had never reciprocated interested in the many heads she'd turned and remained a Leek in name and spirit.

"You know why we had to," Cordelia said defensively. "We are under attack."

"That is certainly your opinion," Imogene replied neutrally. "I dare say the rest of the family is less than convinced," she casually remarked, conveniently removing herself from taking sides in this particular debate.

Cordelia turned dramatically to face Imogene. "The rest of the family aren't as good at the old ways as I am! There was a pall upon young Asher, and I mean to find out what it was." Her dark brown eyes were ablaze, not the wild passion of impetuous youth, but the ardent conviction that came with a lived life.

"Someone has done us ill, and I aim to repay it tenfold."

There were many things Imogen could say to that, but they'd all been said. She had lived with Cordelia long enough to know that when her sister-in-law decided upon something, there wasn't any way of talking her out of it. She considered wheeling herself to a more serene section of the room, but such a thing didn't exist. Every corner was occupied by a Leek, here at the behest of Cordelia. It was amazing how small and frenetic a room became when one crammed twelve discontent people inside.

Imogen smoothed her skirt and returned to her book. It was bad enough that she broke her left tibia in the conservatory last weekend—thank goodness the house had an elevator!—but now she had to attend to this charade, no doubt a paranoid manifestation of grief over young Asher. "As you like, Cordelia," she replied to keep the peace. If she could not soothe the beast, better not to give it cause to bite.

Cordelia looked out the window again, singularly focused on the long, winding drive that led to Buttercrambe. Imogene couldn't decide if her sister-in-law was blind or deliberately indifferent to how her actions affected the family, but she saw no point in giving the issue another thought. It wouldn't change Cordelia's course. She was a juggernaut, and one did not have to practice the arts to sense the strength of her will.

The flash of a headlight drew her attention, and the matriarch donned a fierce smile. Cordelia reflexively touched the string of pearls around her neck, an heirloom passed down from her mother. She was going to get to the bottom of this. No one attacked a Leek and got away with it. She ceremoniously announced for the benefit of the others, "I believe he's arrived."

*****

Wilson followed the directions from his phone and gently steered his rented BMW down an unmarked road. He slowed down to maneuver the curves and, after a particularly tortuous turn, found himself driving toward Buttercrambe Hall. The pictures had not done it justice; it was majestic, even in the brutal rain. He pulled around to the back and the grand porte-cochère where two men were waiting for him, staff by the look of their white shirts and black suits. The first offered to escort him into the house while the second deftly slid into the driver's seat to park his car in the distant garage, retrieve his luggage, and take it to his room.

A massive metal shield was affixed to the solid wooden exterior doors, emblazed with the Leek family coat of arms: three golden rampant unicorns on a black field. The shield split in half as the butler opened the door and bid Wilson to follow him inside. Unlike his younger counterpart that was on his way to the garage, the butler filled his starched uniform with pride as he strode down the smaller passage into an impressive hallway, his back stiff enough to shame a brace.

Wilson followed, mentally orienting himself from the rear entrance and noting the different junctions and doorways not taken. There was no chatter between them as they traveled, only the perfunctory inquiry: how would sir like to be introduced?

"Mr. David Wilson," the butler intoned after he opened the door into the Grand Chamber. It felt odd going by Wilson, but the Salt Mine felt it more prudent to use a name that was tied to official agencies than one of his other alias—better the Leeks not know how extensive the Mine's reach was, should they decide to investigate privately.

The butler stepped back to the side of the door and melted into the background, leaving Wilson exposed at the threshold. The languid majesty of the room and the faces of the Leeks within hit him all at once, and he felt like he'd stumbled upon a scene in an Agatha Christie mystery. He stepped out of the marble antechamber and into his role.

Cordelia broke from the pack and greeted him, "Welcome to Buttercrambe Hall, Mr. Wilson." She held out her hand and was a little surprised when he accepted it properly instead of trying to shake it like a Yank.

"Thank you for the invitation, Lady Leek. Were that it could be under better circumstances," he replied politely. He felt her will and keen eyes wash over him. He kept his guard intact against her probe but made no move to counterattack—he only had one chance to make a first impression, and much could be gleaned by how she wielded her will.

There was no doubt in his mind that Cordelia had the run of the roost, even though she was not born a Leek. The way she purported herself spoke volumes, as did how the rest of the family waited for her assessment of him. She hailed from a distinguished magical family in her own right, albeit one whose means had faltered after the Second World War. Money may fade, but not breeding. Whoever she used to be, she was a Leek now.

Satisfied with her initial impressions, the matriarch made a friendly gesture. "Things are what they are, Mr. Wilson. Let me introduce the family." Wilson put current faces to names as she ran through the members of the house. By the time they were through with introductions, the servants had tea ready and they adjourned further into the Grand Chamber.

The room was so large, there were several separate sitting areas, and Cordelia indicated that Wilson should join her, Imogen, Marmaduke, and Vavasour before the grand fireplace. The other family members spread out and returned to whatever diversions they'd been doing before his arrival. There was no question of leaving, even if they were not called to speak to Wilson directly.

Marmaduke Durand Leek was tall like his mother, with a strong chin and symmetrical face. Asher had taken after him, down to his blond hair, blue eyes, and thin lips. Everything about Marmaduke was quintessentially English; he knew no other way to be. Were it not for the naive sincerity underpinning the entirety of it, Wilson would have thought it an act.

His wife, however, was decidedly French in appearance. Her face was striking, with smoldering, deep-set brown eyes, an aquiline nose, and a slight olive tint underlying her fair complexion. She wore light but effective makeup, and her short auburn was styled simply but chic. Dressed in Breton stripes with a red scarf tied around her neck, non-stretch denim, and black leather ankle boots, she would be indistinguishable from the swathes of women having a coffee and a smoke in any Parisian cafe. The only hint of her South African background was the slight accent in her spoken English and her preference for Vetamite over Marmite.

It was Imogene who broke the uncomfortable silence, making comment on the wretched weather and inquiring on his travel in such conditions. He reassured her he was quite used to dreary cold weather, and made remarks about the beauty of the estate—as much as he had seen on the drive up. Noting the book in her lap, Wilson made reference to the libraries, and she beamed at the prospect of showing another avid reader their prized First Folio.

"I'm sure Mr. Wilson will want to get straight to business," Cordelia addressed her sister-in-law before turning to Wilson. "What are your plans, Mr. Wilson?"

Wilson set his teacup on its saucer and met her sharp inquiry. "You have approached us with concerns of foul play, so I'll be treating this as a murder investigation." Cordelia smugly nodded her head—finally, someone was taking this seriously.

"And what exactly does that entail?" Vavasour asked. "It's been a trying time. I'm not sure how much more of this I can take."

Wilson tilted his head sympathetically. "I will need to investigate Asher's life to find points of connection with peculiar aspects of his death. That means interviewing the family members, staff, and any close personal friends of his."

"So you'll be digging for dirt on our son," Marmaduke asserted.

"I need a clear picture of who your son was in order to find out who killed him, especially if magic was used," Wilson tactfully replied. "Additionally, I'll need to explore the quality and type of wards on the house and Asher's residence while he was at university."

"Why would you need investigate the wards?" Imogene wondered aloud.

"If Asher was killed using magic, knowing what sort of protections were in place—and were ultimately lacking—would help narrow the field," Wilson gave plausible reasoning. "There have been other university students who have recently died in a similar fashion as Asher. None of them studied at Manchester University nor were students of history like Asher, but I will also be investigating that angle as well."

"And how long do you think this will take?" Cordelia reasserted herself in the conversation.

"The part of the investigation under our control shouldn't take more than a few days," Wilson responded. Cordelia liked his choice of pronoun.

"Good. While you're here, don't hesitate to avail yourself of anything you need," the countess said. "I've informed the family to be as helpful as they can, and Taylor"—she looked at the butler who had seen Wilson into the house—"will see to your every need, and answer questions regarding the daily activities of Buttercrambe Hall."

Wilson leaned in and squared up with Marmaduke and Vavasour. "I'd like to start by asking you a few questions. I've read the coroner's report and your statements contained in the police report, but I know there are things you couldn't tell them about your son. What kind of practitioner was he? Did he show a talent or preference for any particular esoteric field?"

They looked to each other first, and then to Cordelia. "Oh, go on and tell him, Daunty. It's nothing I don't already know," she chided her only son.

Marmaduke nodded and spoke in euphemistic terms, "Our son was an extremely intelligent young man, but he wasn't what one would call talented in the arts. He struggled to master the basics and was an absolute train wreck at summoning, but he was quite good at scrying."

"He had a remarkable memory," Vavasour explained; scrying involved casting one's consciousness to another location and relied on remembering a place or object in great detail.

"Unfortunately, he mostly used it to memorize historical trivia. He wasn't much interested in his powers and barely practiced when he was here. As far as I know, he wasn't practicing at school."

"So everyone in the family is a practitioner?" Wilson asked. While the Salt Mine had a full genealogy, such information was lacking.

Cordelia clipped out a terse, "Everyone."

"Even the spouses?" Wilson queried for completeness.

"Especially the spouses," she said emphatically. "Do you think the line's just going to serendipitously continue without careful tending?"

"Mother," Marmaduke injected. "You said to be honest with Mr. Wilson."

The statement hung in the air until Cordelia worried that the silence around the fireplace would draw the attention of the others. "Well, Ferris is a bit of a late bloomer," she admitted, "but we're still holding out hope."

Marmaduke scoffed, and Wilson held his tongue and let the scene unfold. "He's not a late bloomer, Mother, and you know it. He's a bungle, a candling, a damp squib—"

"Watch your tongue," Imogene spoke sharply. "He's still a Leek." Cordelia's eyes darted to her sister-in-law, and the older women shared a glance and understanding.

"Yes, he is a Leek. One without the talent," Marmaduke doubled down. "And if you didn't want to divulge the unsavory family secrets, you shouldn't have invited this American here. Either let Mr. Wilson do his job or send him home, because my patience wears thin. Asher is gone, and none of us can move on as long as you persist with this obsession," he growled.

The entire room turned quiet at the explosive rawness from the otherwise reserved man.

Cordelia abided her son's blows and spoke instead to Wilson. "Do you have children, Mr. Wilson?" Wilson shook his head. "I applaud your sensibility. Children are nothing but a difficulty until they grow old enough to thoroughly disappoint you."

With that, Marmaduke rose to his feet. "Fine, Mother. Have it your way. You always do, regardless how it affects the rest of us. But Mr. Wilson will get the whole story from me, if for no other reason than to embarrass you." He held out his hand to his wife. "Coming dear?" Vavasour took his hand and together they strode out of the Grand Chamber. Sensing an opportunity for escape from familial duty, Ferris and Millicent followed their parents.

"Don't mind them, Mr. Wilson. They've been under a lot of stress," Imogen tried to patch up the hole left with their departure. "They know something strange is afoot, but they didn't want outside involvement. Your presence reminds them of the gravity of their loss."

"Of course," Wilson responded. "Perhaps it would be better for me to start with the house and interview them later in private."

"As you like, Mr. Wilson," Cordelia assented. She raised her hand and voice, "Taylor!" The butler instantly approached. "Please escort Mr. Wilson around the estate."

"Yes, my lady," Taylor replied in a deferential tone mastered via years of service. He was of indeterminable age, but Wilson guessed at least late forties from the receding hairline and distinguished hint of gray. "Would sir like to start at the front entrance?" he skillfully phrased his suggestion as a question. Wilson couldn't let such understated excellence go unrewarded, and he let Taylor lead the way.

The front entrance was a pair of oversized double doors; they were smaller than Wilson had expected for such a grand house, but perhaps it was more majestic from the outside. The rain was steadily coming down, but it had lost most of its fierceness. The rib-vaulted bricks just outside of the door created another porte-cochère, granting them some cover. Next to the door was an elephant's foot umbrella holder made of wrought iron, just below the polished brass handle that connected to a distant doorbell within.

"The house protections include the porte-cochère, Mr. Wilson," Taylor informed him as he retrieved an umbrella wide enough for the two of them. He led Wilson to the exterior pillars where the soft rain pattered against the taut fabric.

"Are all of the staff aware of them?" Wilson asked.

"Those of us who've been in service for a sufficient time know." Wilson's raised eyebrow enticed him to add, "I've been here for fifteen years, sir"

"Are you or any of your colleagues practitioners?" Wilson queried.

"Not that I'm aware of, sir," the butler answered with precision. That was congruent with the Mine's files, but Wilson would still check for himself. There were numerous ways to test for magical aptitude, and his preferred method was to create an auditory illusion that could only be heard by practitioners. Sounds could be ignored, but if it was something sudden and jarring—like someone dropping a tray of glasses—a reaction would be almost reflexive.

Wilson gathered his will—*think, think, think*—and found the perimeter of the wards. "Well then, let's get started," he said aloud as he pulled his jacket closer and started walking the perimeter of the hall. Taylor effortlessly stayed lockstep with him, shielding him from the bulk of the drizzle.

Chapter Seven

Joule Library, Manchester, Greater Manchester, UK
3rd of December, 5:45 p.m. (GMT)

Ferris Leek caught himself rereading the same paragraph a third time, none of it sinking in any better on this pass. He reached for the extra-large coffee he'd brought with him, only to find it drained. Even though there were clocks on the wall, he grabbed his phone to check the time out of habit.

It was a ninety-minute drive with no traffic back to Buttercrambe Hall, but if he left now, he would be in the thick of rush hour. The chance of him making it back for dinner was slim to none. He sent off a quick message to his mother, letting her know he'd lost track of time studying and not to expect him for dinner.

He knew what it must look like, but he really did need to study. The semester was almost over and he'd been falling behind in almost all of his classes. The school had offered him time off for bereavement, but Ferris had chosen to press on. His studies gave him purpose, and it filled the emptiness left by his brother's absence. He just had to get through this next ten days; then there would be no more new material and he'd have a month to cram for exams.

His phone buzzed with her reply: *Don't be too late. Don't forget to eat something. Love you.* She had taken to ending all her texts like that, ever since Asher's death. It would have drove Asher nuts. He would have found it cloying, but Ferris didn't mind. He texted back *<3 u 2* and put his phone away. He rifled through his backpack and pulled out a sheet of caffeine pills, popping one out of the foiled blister pack and chasing it down with his water bottle. It would take a minute to kick in, but it would keep him going. The library didn't close for another two hours.

Joule Library consisted of floors D, E and F of the Sackville Street Building, the former campus of the University of Manchester Institute of Science and Technology (UMIST) before it merged with Victoria University of Manchester in 2004 to form the University of Manchester. While much of the interior had been renovated for modern use, the actual building was a grade II historic building constructed with Burmantofts terracotta. It was a stalwart edifice dedicated to science and technology, sitting at the heart of Manchester's city center.

It was one of Ferris's favorite places to study. The juxtaposition of the soft study seating and utility carpeting amidst the majesty of the Sackville Street Building's original foyer and exterior suited him. He liked that it was mostly engineering students here instead of the mix found at the main campus library. He was amused that it was named after the mathematician and physicist James Prescott Joule—as in the unit of energy and the first law of magnetostriction—except he was a brewer by profession and science was only his hobby. It had taken Ferris the better part of last year to find his nook on the second floor of the library, and it was the first place he checked for an empty seat each time he came.

Technically, he didn't need to be on campus to study, He had online access to all the journals and references he needed for his final papers, and he wasn't working on his build today, but it was the perfect excuse to get out of Buttercrambe Hall and away from his family for a few hours. Going back did lessen his perception of Asher's absence. It was easier to forget he was gone for brief stints of time with more people and space to fill the void. In an estate as large as Buttercrambe Hall, not seeing or hearing Asher wasn't nearly so out-of-place as it was in their shared flat in Manchester.

Asher could have gone anywhere for his PhD, but he choose the University of Manchester just about the time when Ferris was applying to universities. They had never spoken about it, but he knew Asher was doing him a solid. It made their grandmother's and parents' objection to Ferris pursuing engineering at the former UMIST—an institution that had produced no less than twenty Nobel laureates—that much harder to make. Wasn't his big brother already there to look after him? Now, he was never going to be able to thank him for that.

Ferris felt the caffeine start to kick in, and he dove back into his water engineering textbook. His eyes narrowed and his mind focused. This time, the paragraph made a little more sense, as did the diagram opposite it. When Ferris applied to the University of Manchester's Department of Mechanical, Aerospace, and Civil Engineering, he was unaware of the different certifications and specializations within engineering. All he knew was that he wanted to build real, physical things—big things—much to the consternation of his grandmother.

She'd just assumed he and Asher would go into finance and then straight into the family business. It was bad enough that Asher wanted to go into history, but Ferris studying something other than finance too? She had a lot of plans for the Durand Leek brothers. After university, Asher would marry a practitioner from an influential family, and if Asher's mate was light on funds, Ferris would marry someone for money. It all fit together so neatly, except no one had consulted the brothers.

There was a time when Ferris had envied his older brother for having the arcane talent, but over time he'd grown to understand it was also a chain tethering Asher to Buttercrambe Hall and familial duty. Perhaps that was why Asher was so adamant about studying history—if the rest of his life was to be sacrificed for the greater Leek good, at least he could follow his passion mentally. Either way, that initial crack in the family's plans spiraled, making the way easier for Ferris.

With the help of his academic advisor, Ferris figured out he wanted to become a civil engineer. It didn't make as much as the other branches, but that wasn't as important a consideration for him. He just wanted to do something he felt was worthwhile. While he'd done well enough on his GCSEs and A levels to qualify for a four-year MEng program, he wasn't certain *what kind* of civil engineering he wanted to study. Fortunately, he didn't have to know right off the bat; the goal of all first year civil engineering student was the same: survive and pass all the core classes.

But now that he in his second year, he had to start making decisions. If he wanted to pursue structural civil engineering, he needed to start taking different classes. Did he want to go four years for a masters of engineering or call it quits after three with a bachelor's degree? What about extra courses for management training or a year working in the industry as part of his education? Having actual work experience would give him a leg up on other new graduates.

His advisor had laid out his options and told him the most important thing was to figure out what he wanted to do when he finished school. Once he knew that, his advisor could make sure he had the right classes and cluster of letters after his name when he graduated. He had also advised Ferris that there was nothing wrong with taking some time off after Asher's death—he wouldn't even be behind his peers since he hadn't taken a gap year.

Ferris was eyeball deep in a schematic that spanned two

spreads when a chime came over the loudspeaker, breaking the silence of the quiet study area. "The library will be closing in thirty minutes. Please wrap up your studies accordingly," the feminine voice echoed through the stacks. He looked up and confirmed the time. He'd be lying if he said all this wasn't affecting his concentration, but the caffeine helped. At the moment, he wasn't at risk of failing any of his classes, but engineering classes weren't fire-and-forget. Future courses were built on the knowledge gained in previous ones, and it didn't take an engineer to understand how important a foundation was to a structure.

Ferris took one last look at the diagram before shutting the tome and packing up. Backpack slung over one shoulder, he tossed his empty coffee cup into the wastebasket on his way to the stairs. His footfalls echoed in the stairwell and he slowed his pace when he entered the original foyer with its black and white checkered floor. He liked to cross between the rows of carved columns while only stepping on the black tiles, like his own private game of hopscotch. Making it look like part of his normal gait was half the fun.

He hadn't realized how late it had gotten or how hungry he was until he stepped out into the cold, dark night. They would be done with dinner by now; he could return to Buttercrambe Hall, sneak into the kitchen and forage for leftovers in peace. His stomach growled its objection at the delay, and he headed to a nearby cafe with wifi that served food and coffee. If it weren't for the hunting trip tomorrow, he would have stayed in the flat he and Asher shared in Manchester, but he couldn't leave his cousin Basil to suffer their older cousin Grant alone.

He found a seat in a cozy corner and claimed it before anyone else could take it. Then, he put in an order for food and drink and checked his phone while he waited.

Chapter Eight

Buttercrambe Hall, Yorkshire, UK
3rd of December, 8:15 p.m. (GMT)

Wilson climbed the stairs to the third floor, where Lady Leek had set him up for the night. It was spacious and richly decorated with a fantastic view of the massive front lawn bisected by the black asphalt driveway. In the misty haze of the evening fog, the twin canon obusier de 12—or 12-pounder Napoleon, as it was called in the United States—cast long ominous shadows. While those weapons were largely decorative in nature, Buttercrambe Hall was far from defenseless.

The perimeter sweep of the house had revealed antiquated wards. Based on their configuration and choice of runes, Wilson was fairly certain they hadn't changed since before the First World War. Although they were old, they were powerful and the family hadn't been lax in maintaining them.

The level of craft needed to create a robust magical ward was exponentially greater than that required to sustain it, and all it took was one member of the family with above-average practice to put a strong ward into place. Then, anyone who able to wield magic could power it with their will with minimal training. Like wealth, old magical families had the cumulative benefits of the generations, but only if they held onto their esoteric abilities.

The technological defenses were present but on the whole, outdated. Most of the house's security functioned on a CCTV system that might have been old enough to remember disco, although it had been "upgraded" at some point to record to CDs rather than VCR, as it had previously. During his tour of the Hall with Taylor—both interior and exterior—he'd carefully noted the location, type, and relative age of all cameras.

There were only two places that were up to Wilson's standard and therefore off limits unless absolutely required: the library that contained the newly discovered First Folio, and the antechamber to the family's magical vault located in a secret basement in the middle of the house. The cameras were the same model and probably installed at the same time. The former was most likely a requirement of the insurance company who held the policy and the later protected nothing less than the Leek magical legacy. Wilson would have loved to take a peek at what was inside their vault, and not for the first time, he envied Mau's abilities.

Then, he'd spent much of the late afternoon interviewing most of the resident Leeks individually, away from the prying eyes of the countess. Wilson encouraged them to speak freely and honestly, but none of them could shed much light on Asher's cryptic last words or about his personal life. He expected such unawareness from his parents, aunts, and uncles, but cousins and siblings tended to be more nosey. Then again, Asher was older than all of them and what twenty-one-year-old confided in their sixteen-year-old sister or cousin? Wilson held out hope that Ferris, Asher's younger brother and school flatmate, would be a better font of information, but he had taken off before dinner.

The food was exceptional but the atmosphere charged. It was obvious that the Leeks had difficulties tolerating each other at the best of times, but they put on a family dinner for Wilson despite Ferris's absence. He'd picked up an invitation from Grant FitzAlan Leek to go birding tomorrow morning to bag a few more grouse before the season ended. The redhead was a tall man that was once muscular but had slid into late-middle-aged fatness. He drank too much, spoke too loud, and laughed too readily at his own "jokes." He would have declined, but Ferris was supposed to be in attendance and he welcomed a chance to speak to him away from his nuclear family.

Wilson loosened his tie and allowed himself to relax once he closed the door to his bedroom. He typically played observant wallflower in social scenarios, but the Leeks kept engaging him into conversation: asking questions about his profession, the state of things in America, and digging for information other family members may have revealed. He'd held his own, but it was exhausting. He didn't know how Clover did it all the time as a matter of course. He would choose walking the perimeter in the rain with the butler over another Leek family meal any day of the year.

As if on cue, Taylor knocked on his door. Wilson had made plans to see Asher's room after dinner while the Leeks were occupied in their postprandial squabbling. The butler escorted him through the hallways to Asher's suite, composed of two rooms and a bathroom that connected with Ferris's rooms. The front room was like a mini-living room, filled with comfortable, well-used furniture placed around a giant television hooked up with several gaming consoles. The actual bedroom contained an antique four-poster bed and a hodgepodge of furniture: an early Victorian chest of drawers, a Regency wardrobe, a late Victorian closed-shelf bookcase, and a battered Arts & Crafts desk facing the window.

Once Wilson had the lay of the land, he addressed the butler, "Taylor, I'm curious. What did you think of Asher?"

His face and posture didn't change, but Wilson knew his question was being weighed. They had spent the better part of the afternoon together, and while they were both here at the behest of the Leeks, Wilson was far from hired help and Taylor, for better or for worse, had spent most of his life in service.

"Mr. Asher was a driven young man," he carefully chose his words. "When he decided to embark on a task, he did so with his full focus—sometimes burning the candle at both ends, as they say." The omission of the obligatory "sir" told Wilson that Taylor was on the level.

"I see. And were you aware of anything he was involved with that he didn't want his parents or grandmother to know?"

"Nothing out of the ordinary for a young man his age," Taylor replied after a moment of hesitation. He brushed past Wilson to the desk and removed the front drawer, revealing a small hidden compartment. His nimble fingers produced a metal cigarette case.

Wilson appreciated the heft of it in his hand. It was an old, substantial thing with a whaling scene etched into the pewter. Inside, he found a small amount of marijuana in a plastic bag, a dozen pills that looked like MDMA, and two flat blister-packed sheets. The first was 200 mg caffeine pills and the second 325 mg aspirin tablets.

"I understand concealing the party pills and pot, but why was he hiding caffeine pills and aspirin?" Wilson puzzled.

"Lady Leek does not approve of any non-prescribed medications in the house after an unfortunate accident with her brother, especially anything for pain," Taylor informed him. Wilson recalled from the files a younger brother that died of an overdose of barbiturates that was deemed accidental, but the Mine believed it was a hushed-up suicide.

"Not even aspirin?" Wilson balked.

"She doesn't even allow vitamins," Taylor replied. Wilson thought he could hear just the hint of exasperation in his otherwise level tone.

Wilson repacked the contraband into the case and put it

back in its hiding place. "We all have our secrets," he said as he slid it back into the niche and gently slid the drawer back into its slot. Taylor almost smiled. "If you wouldn't mind, Taylor, I need some privacy for the next step of the investigation. Trade secrets."

The butler's impassive bearing returned. "I'll be outside, sir," Taylor replied, status quo restored.

Wilson waited until he heard the click of the door to salt, starting with the bedroom. As he waited for the salt to do its magic, he perused the books on the shelves. At first glance, it looked like most of the titles were purely decorative. Wilson suspected Asher wasn't reading Heinrich von Kleist's *Das Käthchen von Heilbronn* or Georg Wilhelm Friedrich Hegel's *Differenz des Fichteschen und Schellingschen Systems der Philosophie* in their native tongue, as there was no indication that he'd ever learned German. However, there were a few history titles that were definitely Asher's—Madhusree Mukerjee's *Churchill's Secret War: The British Empire and the Ravaging of India during World War II* and Cain and Hopkins's *British Imperialism 1688-2015* caught Wilson's attention. Asher's degree was in ancient history, but he obviously had some interests in more-recent events.

Normally, he would look for discrepancies in the dust to determine which books saw more use, but the lack of any denied him such insight. Even the small spaces behind the books on the shelves were spotless. That level of cleaning required removing each book during dusting, which suggested one of two things: utter dedication on Buttercrambe Hall's staff or the real cleaning crew was of the magical persuasion. It wasn't unusual for old magical families to acquire a cleaning faerie or two over the generations.

The salt shook into a fuzzy but predominate signature by the desk; more than likely it was Asher's, but Wilson could only confirm that after salting his Manchester residence. A practitioner gave a crisper signature the more time they spent at a location, and according to his parents, Asher hadn't been to Buttercrambe Hall since his last break at university.

There were a few other faint signatures around the room bearing a resemblance to Asher's, but distinct in their own right. Wilson chalked it up to Asher's parents or grandmother using magic in the room sometime after his death. The study of magical signatures within familial lines was one of Chloe's interests, the esoteric equivalent of inheriting similar physiologic features. He took pictures of everything and kicked the salt to break the magic, dispersing and grinding the fine white dust into the carpet.

Wilson salted the bathroom and media room with similar results, and he considered tossing the area in a thorough search but decided against it. It would have been different if he was first on the scene immediately after Asher's death, but the suite had already been sanitized. All his clothes were hung and folded with care, there were two sets of toiletries in the bathroom, and his console games were lined up neatly on the shelves. Wilson had seen it before; sometimes it took families a while to put away their loved one's things for good, and a physical search would just make a mess for the staff to clean, be it mundane or magical.

Wilson opted for an enhanced esoteric sweep. He locked the door to the suite and the bathroom to ensure he wasn't disturbed. He opened as many drawers and cabinets as he could while still maintaining visibility of the contents within. He even unearthed the cigarette case and placed it on top of the desk. Then, he pulled out the hag stone from his pocket.

He started the count as soon as he put it to his right eye—*one*... *two*... *three*... The room lost much of its color, becoming a dull pastel version of its real self. He started in the bathroom, looking for anything that illuminated through the stone. When no vibrant colors presented themselves, Wilson moved into the bedroom and looked over that area.

He pulled the hag stone away just before the count of ten and closed the spaces he'd already cleared. He sent out a thread of his will to check the bedroom before attempting a second pass. The fabric of reality seemed intact, and he raised the stone to his eye again, this time opening the drawers he hadn't visually scanned yet. Again, nothing seemed esoteric, which struck Wilson as odd.

From his experience, magical families generally had more permissive use of magic to varying degrees. The valuable, rare, or dangerous stuff was almost always in the vault, but small magics that conferred convenience were typically left out in the open: a pen that never needed ink, a magical lighter so one need never worry about refueling, or a clasp that never broke. Perhaps such things were not entrusted to the children, but Asher was twenty-one and at university pursuing his PhD. He was hardly a child anymore. Wilson was beginning to wonder if the family had already removed enchanted familial items given to Asher, or if they were at his Manchester residence.

Wilson moved to the front room and made his third and final pass; unsurprisingly, Asher's TV and games were not magical. He returned the stone to his pocket as he walked back to the bathroom and covered his trail. A quick wipe with a damp piece of toilet paper took care of the salt on the bathroom floor and he unlocked the door adjoining Ferris's suite. He tested the door and found it locked from Ferris's side. Were Taylor not waiting for him in the hall, he would have considered picking the lock and taking a look see.

He stepped back into the bedroom and put things back in order. *Bedroom—check*, Wilson ticked off his mental list. When he came to the front room, he realized he didn't know what to call it. There was no such thing as a media room when the house was built and a game room wouldn't be attached to private quarters. He unlocked the door and popped his head out. "Taylor?" he beckoned.

The butler emerged from the side of the door. "Yes, sir,"

"What do you call this room? The one with the TV."

"It's a dressing room, sir."

"Dressing room?"

"It's where one's valet would dress a gentleman."

Wilson uttered the sound of his curiosity being sated. "Ah! Thank you. That was bugging me. I should be done shortly."

"Of course, sir."

As Wilson checked the nooks and crannies of the dressing room, he pondered the picture of Asher Leek that was coming into focus: a highly intelligent and driven young man who wasn't averse to enjoying life. A practitioner who wasn't much interested in magic and didn't have the most basic of esoteric supplies in his childhood bedroom. A person who had garnered enough respect from the servants that they were unwilling to betray his secrets to Lady Leek or his parents. It was a start.

"I think I've got everything I need for tonight," Wilson said as he exited the suite. "Thank you for your help, Taylor."

"Certainly, sir." The butler led him back to his room—no doubt at the behest of Cordelia, who didn't want the American running loose and unsupervised in her domain. "Have a good evening, sir," he said as he deposited Wilson at his quarters.

"And you as well, Taylor," Wilson bid him as he closed the door between them.

He pantomimed readying for bed, examining his room for cameras along the way. Once he was reasonably sure there were none, he checked for microphones with his electric shaver that doubled as both a radiofrequency detector and as a non-linear junction detector. The NLJD gave off several positives, each of which were false when Wilson excluded them individually. Then, he turned off all the lights and used his flashlight's black light and infrared mode to make sure that nothing unusual popped up in those spectrums.

Finally certain that he wasn't under observation, Wilson set his alarm and climbed into bed. The frame was a heritage piece, but the mattress was modern and quite comfortable. The radiator was warm to the touch and the duvet was thick and fluffy. He loaded up the next episode of the documentary about the Habsburg Empire he'd started in Detroit and watched until he was tired enough to catch a few hours of sleep.

Chapter Nine

Buttercrambe Hall, Yorkshire, UK
4th of December, 2:00 a.m. (GMT)

Wilson woke to the vibrating alarm of his phone. Getting up in the middle of the night to do surveying and bugging sounded like a good idea yesterday, but now, he was less convinced of its wisdom. The plush bed was so warm and the room so chilly. After a few deep breaths, he pushed back the covers.

He listened to the darkened house for sounds of activity but found it blissfully quiet. Then he went to the window, checking to make sure no one was moving about outside. With Buttercrambe Hall tucked in for the night, Wilson went to work. He dressed in black, with soft-soled shoes and thin burglar's gloves, and then emptied his mostly unpacked luggage, including his Glock from the concealed compartment. Then, he moved the carry-on to the Sheraton chair at the writing desk overlooking one of the large windows and secured it to the back of the chair with extra shoestrings, brought specifically for that purpose.

The cold stung as he opened the window, but thankfully,

the wind was tame. He held fast to the seat and pushed the back of the chair out of the window, ensuring the attached luggage left the warded area of the Hall. Tucking a chair leg under each arm, he turned the dials on the tumblers: 1776, 1989, 2001. He felt the pop reverberate through the chair as the case expanded and the legs dug into his armpits at the increased weight. He smiled at the physical confirmation that the exchange was complete.

Wilson pulled the chair back inside and carefully set it down on the carpet before closing the window. He unlocked the suitcase that had just been inside the 500 and carefully unpacked his gear. He'd liberated the first item from an Ivory Tower agent two years ago and had been itching to use since, but never had the occasion: a LiDAR designed for architectural surveying.

Short for Light Detection and Ranging, a LiDAR used lasers to map a space in all three dimensions—much like sonar did with sound, but much better. If everything went according to plan, the Salt Mine would have better schematics of Buttercrambe Hall than the Leek family, complete with room labels, notes, and locations of bugs placed during his visit. Just the thought of it made Wilson smile.

First things first, Wilson did a gear check. He'd tested it at the 500 before he'd left town, but he didn't know if teleportation between coterminous extradimensional spaces affected precision technology. The LiDAR came in three pieces.

The largest component was a bulky black backpack that housed the power supply and recording device. The second piece was a cylindrical rod that reminded him of a WWI stick grenade, but it was too important to throw and yell "fire in the hole," even in jest, although it crossed his mind. The rod sent and received the laser whose data would be used to generate a map. It attached to the extendable pole on the top of the backpack, allowing the wearer to simply walk where he wanted to survey. The final part was a hand-held monitor no bigger than a cell phone.

He plugged in all the cables and fired it up. Much to his relief, the unit lit up and an image of his room immediately appeared on the screen. He moved the rod around his person, making sure the monitor reflected the obstruction he'd placed in its path. Satisfied with his rudimentary triage, Wilson shut it down to save the battery and affixed the rod to the backpack.

The other piece of equipment in the case was a handheld ground penetrating radar designed for use in construction. If he detected any unusual dimensions with the LiDAR that were suggestive of a hidden room, he'd use the radar unit to suss out what was behind the walls themselves.

Then, he did a systematic inventory of his other gear, putting them in specific pockets for immediate and precise retrieval: a cluster of Weber's new long-lasting bugs, his saltcaster and phone, the hag stone, the true Gomeda, and a pen needle. He kept Andvaranaut on the chain around his neck so he could slip it on his finger if he felt like it was needed.

He hoisted the LiDAR on his back and pulled the slack out of the straps so the unit wouldn't sag and capture the back of his head. He slung the ground penetrating radar over his neck and shoulder for fast retrieval should he hit pay dirt on the first pass. The idea was to walk everywhere he and Taylor had gone earlier in the day—with the exception of the basement leading to the family vault and the library housing the First Folio. The magical and mundane security there would need a little more consideration and planning to circumvent. That would be for a later expedition.

Wilson switched on the LiDAR again, hit record, and started with his room. He ungloved his left hand and held the pen needle against the tip of his fourth finger. A fat weal of blood formed as he held pressure proximal to the digit, and he applied it to the true Gomeda. Suddenly, the world seemed thinner. The large mirror on the wall confirmed the complete disappearance of Wilson and the possessions on his person. Even the light of the LiDAR was absent.

He quietly opened the door to his room—the stone made him invisible, not silent—and crept through the empty corridor. Most of the areas he'd already walked with Taylor were on the first floor, but since he was already on the third floor, why not start there?

Most of the doors were closed on the third and second floor, and he decided to leave them that way for his first foray.

More than likely, they were bedrooms and until he knew which were occupied and by whom, he didn't want to stumble upon or wake a sleeping Leek. He kept to the carpeted areas as much as possible and avoided the few interior cameras. The beauty of the LiDAR was that he didn't have to fully enter a space to get a decent rendering. Every so often, he reapplied blood to the magical garnet, working his way through the medial and distal aspects of the fingers on his left hand.

He made quick work of the upper floors and descended to the ground floor—the only level with a significant number of open rooms designed for communal family use and various degrees of entertaining visitors. While the LiDAR generated its image, Wilson systematically used the hag stone for cursory sweeps for magic. He mentally marked down anything that indicated as being magical for later investigation.

All houses were spookier at night, and Buttercrambe Hall was no exception. Every sound was amplified by the relative quiet and shadows had more depth, but each time Wilson probed the darkness with his will, he found nothing untoward.

He was halfway through the ground-floor library—the one that didn't house the First Folio—when he noticed something moving on top of one of the interior bookshelves on the LiDAR screen. He immediately stopped and peered at the bookshelf in question, but couldn't see anything in the shadowy room. He looked to the screen again and confirmed that something small was silently scuttling from the near end of the shelf to the far end and then back again.

His eyes glued to the screen, Wilson waited to see if the LiDAR could build an image of it instead of a long blur. Unlike newer, more advanced models, the unit he had didn't have the programming to form three-dimensional images of moving objects. Eventually, it was still for long enough for the machine to create a crisp image of a small winged faerie about a foot tall before it returned to pacing, this time on a different shelf.

Wilson silently exhaled in relief; there weren't any faeries of such size that were real threats. He kept the hag stone tucked away—it would only attract its attention—and stayed very still. He ran through the possibilities and came up with two names; given the location and wards, it was either a house faerie or a winged maker.

House faeries were playful pranksters that old dwellings spontaneously generated from time to time. They were an oddity among fae because they were borne and lived exclusively in the mortal realm. There weren't many of them in North America, but England was crawling with them. It was impossible to ward them out because they were created inside the structure, but a practitioner could put an end to their mischief by putting them under their control or casting them out of the building whereupon they quickly perished.

Winged makers, on the other hand, were faeries from the Land of Fae that were drawn to human dwellings. They were one of the few good-natured fae and inspired one of Grimm's stories, *Die Wichtelmänner*, which had been translated into English as *The Elves and the Shoemaker*. He knew from his assessment of the wards that such a creature could not be inside Buttercrambe Hall unless they'd been allowed or invited by the ward keeper at some point in time.

As Wilson ran through the two types of fae, he realized it had been a while since he'd put a fresh drop of blood on the Gomeda; suddenly becoming visible in front of a faerie was less than ideal. He turned ever so slowly on the thick carpets of the library floor and made his way to the door. He was almost out of the room when the creature called out to him.

"I know you're there. I can't see you, but I hear you. What are you doing in here?" Its voice was high-pitched and squeaky, but velvety at the same time, like the aural equivalent of how eating fresh cheese curds felt in the mouth. The fae's reproach narrowed Wilson's choices and fell in line with what he'd suspected when he searched Asher's room—the Leeks had a winged maker cleaner.

"I'm here under invitation from the ward keeper," he responded truthfully. It was best to always speak the truth to faeries. Wilson watched the LiDAR and saw it silently fly nearer to him and land on one of the reading tables.

"Why can't I see you?" it asked. On the screen, the blur shifted to the left and right, like a dog sniffing the air for a scent.

"Because I don't want you to," he curtly replied.

"That's not an answer," the small fae objected.

"On the contrary, it's the best answer," Wilson responded, knowing it would both annoy and intrigue the diminutive faerie. "To whom do I have the pleasure of speaking?"

"I have been named Dirt Feather," it introduced itself. Wilson noted its deliberate choice of words. "And you?" it probed.

"Like you, I am known by many names," Wilson replied. "But to you, I will be known as liberator."

A shooting blur of activity raced across the LiDAR monitor as the faerie appeared on the edge of the table closest to Wilson. "What do you mean by this?" it asked suspiciously.

"You are far from home; bound here in service. You are forced to hide during the day and clean at night when all the house should be asleep. I have the means to free you, should we come to an agreement," Wilson spoke plainly.

The winged maker heard the truth in his words and blinked into sight. Like all fae, it was handsome in face and form, with iridescent wings that shimmered in the dim light. Its lustrous hair was pulled back in an elaborate but effective knot with braids, and there was just a smudge of dirt on its pert button nose. It was dressed in coveralls with a tiny duster in one hand and an apron of many pockets was tied around its slim waist. "It seems you are familiar with my situation."

"But how are you speaking to me? Are you not to stay silent unless spoken to?" Wilson inquired.

The winged maker puffed out its chest proudly. "I don't see anyone in here. If I address an empty, creaky room, it is hardly my fault that the emptiness chooses to speak back."

"Indeed," Wilson agreed. "Old rooms make noises all of the time. Particularly at night."

The tiny fae wasn't sure if it was being made fun of. "They do," it asserted. It wanted to sound tough, but it just came out as petulant. "Now what is this agreement you speak of?" The tips of Dust Feather's wings were fluttering with excitement despite its best efforts to stay aloof. The prospect of freedom was too tempting. The bond placed upon it more than a hundred fifty years ago prevented it from doing many things, and it desperately hoped the disembodied voice wouldn't ask it to do something it couldn't.

"I have some objects I'd like you to place throughout the Hall," Wilson said. "They're small enough that you can carry them while flying, and they do no harm to those of the house. I want you to put them in rooms where the Leeks discuss business or gather socially, but in places they would never think to look."

"The places that are hard to clean, even for me," it said in comprehension.

"Precisely."

"And if I do this, you set me free of the Leek's bond?" it asked for clarification. A deal with a fae was no small matter for either party.

Wilson rubbed his finger lightly over the Gomeda to make sure the blood was at least still sticky. “There are stipulations. First, you have to turn on the discs when you place them—don’t worry, I’ll tell you how. Second, you have to tell me where you put them. And last, you cannot tell or otherwise communicate anything about me, including but not limited to our agreement, who I am, what I possess, what I have done, what I am doing, or who I associate with. Forever until the end of your days.” He laced his words with his will.

Dirt Feather thought about Wilson’s offer. It seemed overly detailed and specific for something so simple. It felt like a trap, but the little faerie yearned to leave the walls of Buttercrambe Hall. Eventually, it cried out “Deal!” and jumped up and down on the table. The winged maker released a small spurt of its will in an esoteric handshake with Wilson’s. “When do I start?”

Wilson smiled. “Right now.” He pulled out a bug he was carrying and placed it on the table next to Dust Feather. The silvery discs became visible once they left his hand. “When you place them, you must twist them to turn them on. When you are finished, go to my room on the third floor, the one over the house entry facing the front lawn. After you tell me where you placed each of the discs, I’ll free you from your bondage. If I’m not there, wait for me. I won’t be long.”

The faerie defiantly nodded and tossed down its miniature duster. It grabbed the first disc and blinked out of sight. Its silhouette remained on the LiDAR screen, where Wilson watched it fly away.

Chapter Ten

Buttercrambe Hall, Yorkshire, UK
4th of December, 3:45 a.m. (GMT)

Wilson plunked down a dozen bugs, which gave him thirty minutes—an hour tops—to finish his scan of the ground floor before the winged maker finished his task and would expect Wilson to keep his end of the bargain. He wasn't lying when he told Dirt Feather he could free him from the Leek's bond over him, but part of the reason he made the claim was to see if that was really the situation at hand. *First Mau, now Dirt Feather*, he mused as he pricked his finger one last time and continued his surveying.

Fae were fickle creatures subject to flights of fancy and whims, but they were good to their word. The tricky part was using the right words to express the truth behind the language. Unlike devils, who were the very epitome of litigiousness, fae were more interested in the spirit of the law. They put a high merit on veracity, and if you didn't believe what you were saying to a faerie, they wouldn't either.

That wasn't to say faeries were straight shooters. They were slippery with language too, just differently. They would tell you the truth, but not the whole truth. If you didn't choose your phrasing carefully, you could find yourself in a jam, and heaven help you if you didn't follow through with your end of a pact with a faerie. Given their mercurial nature, they could give you a disproportionate amount of trouble for such a transgression.

There was a big difference between a bond and a pact. A pact was an accord or oath entered into by two or more independent entities. It was the responsibility of each party to understand their responsibilities to each other and the stipulations of the covenant before agreeing to it, but everyone always had the option of saying "no" upfront. A bond was one party asserting its will over another. It was a confinement full of obligation, compulsion, and restriction. To a flighty creature like a faerie, nothing chaffed worse than enslavement.

As a master summoner, Wilson was well acquainted with the nuances of binding. The less onerous ones were conditional: do X for me and I will set you free afterward. It was transactional in natural and employed by summoners as protection against the supernatural creatures they called upon for help. Based on how excited the winged maker was at the prospect of freedom, he doubted Dirt Feather had a condition for freedom built into the bond.

The bondholder could always retract the binding, but speaking to the Leeks about their magical cleaning staff was the last thing he wanted to do. It would give away his hand, and there was a decent chance they didn't even know they had one in their employ if the age of the wards was any indication. Unfortunately, there was no tricking a Leek into freeing Dirt Feather; breaking an established bond had to be intentional. It wasn't like accidentally breaking the circle during a summoning, which meant Wilson had to have to think out of the box on this one.

He was still invisible when he opened the door to his room and found Dirt Feather sitting on the apron of the overturned Sheraton chair, legs dangling in midair. It had ditched the apron and restyled its resplendent hair. Even its button nose was no longer soiled. The faerie seemed unconcerned that the door opened and closed on its own, but it did not speak until spoken to this time, just in case this was all a Leek trick.

Normally, he wouldn't have invited the fae to wait in his room, but he had all his gear on his person except for his luggage, and they had a deal—anything it did see could never be communicated. To the core of their being, fae were bond to their word and that was one binding that could not be broken.

"Have you turned on and placed all the discs as stipulated?" Wilson addressed the winged maker.

"Yes," it answered.

"Good. Let me get settled and you can tell me where you put them. Just one minute," he reassured the fae on his way to the restroom.

He closed the door for privacy and put the LiDAR in the dry bathtub. In the sink, he washed off the true Gomeda and his reflection stared back at him once more. He dried it off with a towel before putting it back into his pocket.

When Wilson exited the bathroom, Dirt Feather was pacing on the windowsill, looking out the window. It was startled at Wilson's appearance—it'd grown accustomed to the Leeks and had forgotten how differently hideous humans could be. "Can you really free me?" it asked, suspicion evident in its tone.

"You'll soon find out," Wilson said cryptically. "But first, I need to know where you put each of the silvery discs." He pulled out a notepad and click pen from the desk and left it for the faerie. Figuring out which bug was in which room would be annoying, but nothing the Mine techs and analysts couldn't unravel. Soon, the Salt Mine would have ears on Buttercrambe Hall until the batteries wore out.

Its gossamer wings fluttered delicately as it flew to the desk, where it held the pen in both hands and started furiously writing. Wilson recognized the script as magical fae sigils, which transcended language and had no fixed context. Each individual sign conveyed its meaning via telepathy to ensure there was no chance of miscommunication. It was wonderful to "read" a fae sigil, but transcribing or recording them was a pain in the butt. They were indecipherable except for the original sigils; Wilson had once seen a photograph of a line of fae sigils that was simply the same sign repeated a dozen times in a row—incomprehensible except to its intended reader.

The winged maker's willingness to expend the energy

to scribe them was testament to how eager it was to depart Buttercrambe Hall. Dirt Feather dropped the pen as soon as it was done, not bothering to click it closed. "Home, now!" it ordered.

Wilson ran his finger over the sigils, and each broadcast the relevant data in a strange mix of written, verbal, and visionary communication. Once he knew where they were, he pinged them using his phone to make sure they were working. None of them were currently on—the bugs would only activate when a certain decibel threshold was surpassed—but they returned the all-clear to his query.

"You've done as you swore," Wilson declared. "Now I will do as I have promised." He pulled the necklace bearing Andvaranaut from under his shirt and over his head. He released the ring from the chain and held it in his hand.

Dirt Feather cursed but quietly, lest anyone hear. "That is Andvaranaut! *You* have it?" The fae kicked himself for agreeing so readily—it could have been promoted with such information.

"Your complete silence is the price of your freedom," Wilson reminded the faerie. "And you cannot say what I have asked of you is overtly unfair, considering the lengths it will take to break the Leeks' bond over you." The winged maker begrudgingly conceded the point but pouted nonetheless. On top of the missed opportunity for advancement, it couldn't brag to the other fae that it was freed by none other than Andvari's ring.

Wilson walked to the window and held the ring up to the dim light coming off the exterior lampposts. It was heavy, heavier than gold, and its weight wasn't just physical. He could feel the ring press against everything in the room in anticipation of its use, as if it heard others speak of it.

Dirt Feather hovered near it but dared not touch it, even though the faerie desperately wanted to. "It's beautiful."

"It's deadly," Wilson corrected it. He opened the window and the cold air flooded into the room but the hand holding Andvaranaut stayed eerie warm. "I'm going to put the ring on. When I do so, you need to land on my open hand. I'll then push you outside the boundaries of the house wards and you'll be free." The fae understood and nodded.

Wilson gathered his will—*think, think, think*—and cast it out onto Andvaranaut. The ring pulled on his will and wrapped itself in the thin strands of power. It absorbed them—no, it digested them—and Wilson ruthlessly tamped down the sudden panic that reflexively flared up inside him. *I am the master of my will*, he asserted for both his and the ring's benefit. Although his intent was to metaphysically puff out his chest, the roar of his statement took even him by surprise. Andvaranaut eased up, but he could still feel a slight tug. He steadied himself and slid the ring over his finger.

All I want is to move this faerie outside of the window in secrecy. All I want is to move this faerie outside of the window in secrecy, he repeated like a mantra, blocking out all other thoughts except the task before him. He held his hand up, and he barely felt Dirt Feather—so light was its landing and so heavy was his concentration.

Wilson kept repeating his thought. As he pushed his hand out of window, he felt the wards of the house yield to his hand but not break. It was slipping his hand into a glove of pure will. It reminded him of swimming through a school of fish: they parted before him but the school never wavered in coherency.

When his hand was fully extended outside the wards, Dirt Feather breathed the sweet air of liberty. It performed dainty pirouette and bowed to his mysterious liberator in gratitude before taking off like a shot into the darkness. Wilson withdrew his hand and changed his mantra: *All I want is to take off this ring. All I want is to take off this ring.*

He didn't realize he'd been holding his breath until Andvaranaut was free of his finger. He threaded the necklace through it and placed it around his neck, feeling more comfortable with its unnatural weight but not entirely at ease. He wished Dirt Feather safe passage to the Land of Fae and closed the window.

Deal honored, he shimmied under the bed to access the underside of the box springs as didn't want to chance the noise of moving the heavy mattress. With his utility knife, he sliced a hole in the center and taped the black transmitter amplifier to one of the wooden slats. Once he was sure the transmitter wouldn't slip or rattle, he turned it on. Now the Mine was getting the signal. He spooled out his will and mended the thin slit he'd made. It was unlikely anyone would discover the transmitter until the box springs was thrown out, if then.

He retrieved the LiDAR from the bathroom and repacked his equipment back into his large luggage before exchanging it for his empty carry-on. He sent a message to the Mine with the list of bug locations and the initial LiDAR images. *Not bad for a night's work*, he patted himself on the back as he tucked in for a few hours of sleep.

Chapter Eleven

Buttercrambe Hall, Yorkshire, UK
4th of December, 6:55 a.m. (GMT)

It was still dark out when Wilson descended for breakfast, which, according to custom, was served buffet style rather than table service. The mode of delivery in no way diminished the volume of food on offer. Mounds of toast, eggs, bacon, and fruit with an assortment of spreads both savory and sweet graced the sideboard, and the tea was flowing. The kitchen had even brewed coffee for the visiting American.

The table seemed bare by comparison to yesterday's family dinner, but it gave Wilson more time to observe his hunting companions in greater detail. Grant FitzAlan Leek was in fine form this morning, with his fading red hair slicked back and his appetite hearty—the prospect of bagging birds always put him in high spirits. He piled strips of bacon on his plate in a stack that defied gravity. He was noticeably less inebriated than last night, but only slightly less boorish.

The Mine was uncertain why he and his sister resided at the Hall, being third cousins of the Durand Leeks. While his sister Curwen was a skilled magician in her own right, Grant didn't appear to have a useful profession or talent for the arts, but they did believe he had a substantial drinking and gambling problem.

Basil Vries Leek was more discerning in his food, manners, and conversation. He took dry toast with just a scoop of scrambled eggs, two slices of bacon, and a bowl of fresh fruit with his tea. He ate breakfast as he ate every meal: with knife and fork. He was sparing with the butter and jam on his last wedge of toast, savored with a second cup of tea.

Officially, Basil was an investment banker in the family business, but after his involvement in the fallout after the 2008 financial crisis, he spent much of his time in leisure where the family felt he could do less damage. Dark, slim, and handsome, he made appearances at country fetes and handed out ribbons at community competitions, giving the Leek family a pretty public face.

And then there was Ferris, who was quiet and morose in the way only teenaged boys could be. It was undeniable that he and Asher were brothers—they'd inherited the same cheekbones and nose from their father—but Ferris had his mother's dark hair, coloring, and eyes. The cut of his jaw was more delicate than Asher's or Marmaduke's. It gave the overall impression of perpetual ennui. He even managed to eat sullenly.

Grant did most of the talking, reviewing the itinerary and making off-color comments between greasy bites. Basil would give a perfunctory smile at his older cousin's jabs and jokes that would subtly turn into a smirk and a sideways glance at his nephew, to which Ferris would crack a smile and roll his eyes. If Grant saw, he didn't show it.

After breakfast, they adjourned to the India Room, one of four massive staterooms in the Hall. The farthest from the Grand Chamber, it was the least used, but the four gentlemen headed for it nonetheless as it held the guns. Lavishly decorated with items of the subcontinent, the India Room was a shrine to the old imperial days. In the late eighteenth century, the FitzAlans were deeply involved in the East India Company, and when the British Raj seized control over the subcontinent, the Durands flooded the upper tiers of administration, although none ever achieved Governor-General.

With the FitzAlans in the private import/export business and the Durands in position to give them favorable trade status, they quickly capitalized on familial ties. It was salad days for the Leek clan. In the course of nearly two centuries of involvement in India, both branches of the Leeks raked in the pounds and collected large private collections of Indian works of art.

Wilson paused to admire an intricate tapestry on the wall while the family walked indifferently toward a double-sized rosewood cabinet, inured to the wealth of artifacts on display. Grant unlocked the gun cabinet and swung the doors open, revealing a line of shotguns and rifles neatly stacked within. Ferris was about grab a gun when Basil stopped him with his hand.

"Don't be rude, Ferris. Let's let our guest have first pick. Which do you favor, Mr. Wilson?" Basil asked in a polite tone but there was no doubt in Wilson's mind it was a test that doubled as amusement: watch the foreigner not know things we know.

As they were bird hunting, Wilson ignored the rifles entirely and examined each of the shotguns. He felt the weight of their appraising gaze. "Personally, I'd enjoy the FAMARS Excalibur," he stated, chuffed with the knowledge that of everyone in the room, only he'd held the real Excalibur and that no shotgun, no matter how beautifully decorated and engineered, could ever deserve the name. "But that is based on the assumption that you gentlemen already have claims upon the three Holland & Holland Royals."

Grant barked a laugh and clapped Wilson on the shoulders. "You know your guns, Mr. Wilson. And people," he said, grabbing his weapon of choice; it cost more than most vehicles on the road. "Go on, take the FAMARS." Wilson obliged and stepped aside for the others to claim theirs. Basil silently approved as Wilson did a safety check to ensure it was not loaded and had been cleaned before storage—he'd learned the hard way that a wise man didn't trust someone else to take care of his responsibilities.

The troupe marched to the front exit where the Leek family's Land Rover awaited them. Grant and Basil jostled for the keys, and based on Ferris's expression, Wilson surmised it was a reenactment of a familiar contest that was decided when Basil pointed out that Grant could have a tipple on the way if he drove.

Battle won, Basil slid behind the wheel and offered Wilson the front passenger seat while Ferris and Grant rode in the back. With a full tank of gas, the hunting party left Buttercrambe Hall in its rearview mirror and followed the winding country roads into the North York Moors National Park. Grant kept his window cracked so that he could have a smoke, but the rush of air only brought it back into the car with the added benefit of creating a racket.

"Have you ever been to the moors, Mr. Wilson?" Basil made conversation over the noise of the road and open window.

"Not these, no, but I've been to the Scottish Highlands," he succinctly answered.

"The moors here aren't as wild as the Highlands, but let's not kid ourselves: if you've seen one moor, you've seen them all," Basil quipped, eyes steady on the road.

"Dreadful places," Grant declared from behind Wilson.

"Odd sentiment for a man so eager to arrive there," Wilson stated.

Grant leaned into the middle of the vehicle and beamed a satisfied grin. "Oh, don't confuse my intentions, Mr. Wilson. The moors are dreadful, which is why I believe it's my patriotic duty to bear a weapon into their wilds. Someone has to kill everything that moves in that blasted place. May as well be me." There was just a hint of juniper and coriander on his breath.

"But you have no complaints against them when you are sipping a peaty scotch," Basil snidely remarked. Grant roared in laughter.

"How do you find the moors, Ferris?" Wilson tried to coax him into conversation.

He shrugged his shoulders. "They're half okay if the weather's not bad."

"So half okay is a thing now?" Grant drolly queried.

"There's no such thing as bad weather to the man who dresses properly," Basil inserted himself as a verbal buffer. "No worries, Mr. Wilson, we'll get you properly suited up at the house. Over the years, we've acquired an extensive collection of gear for unexpected visitors. The clothing may be out of date, but cozy and dry is always preferable to being fashionable and miserable, don't you think?"

"I disagree," Grant said before Wilson could speak. "Fashionable and miserable describes most of the women I've come across, and I wouldn't trade a good woman for anything."

"Except for another one," Basil corrected. Grant conceded the point with a tilt of his head, but Ferris just cringed and looked out the window at the dark countryside passing by. It wasn't worth correcting their archaic opinions because they already knew they were in the wrong. That was why they said it and took such pleasure in it.

The Hunting House was situated in the North York Moors National Park, but unlike national parks in the US, quite a bit of it was privately owned. The Leek's parcel—one of the largest in private hands—was thirty miles to the north into the moors. The half-timbered Tudor country house was situated in the center of the plot, situated in one of the stream-valleys and surrounded by a large copse of pine and ash.

It was modest compared to Buttercrambe Hall, but the Leeks were hardly roughing it. From first glance on the gravel drive, Wilson guessed it had at least nine or ten bedrooms squirreled about its three floors, and there were servants awaiting their arrival.

Wanting to make the most of their shooting time—the best time for birding was a few hours after dawn and before dusk—Basil and Grant handed Wilson over to Bevin Gilfillan, the gamekeeper, and took off with one of the dogs. Ferris offered to stay behind and show Wilson the way. The youngest Leek was noticeably more at ease the minute the door had closed behind them.

Wilson put the gamekeeper somewhere in his mid-fifties, but it was hard to say considering how tanned he was from years spent outdoors. No gray touched his jet-black hair, and he was built like a brick—tall, thick, and solid. His hands were calloused and rough, but precise as he sorted through drawers and chests to cobble together an ensemble. Given Wilson's thin frame and short stature, he didn't have much of a selection, but it wasn't anything a good belt couldn't fix.

"Have you ever hunted grouse, Mr. Wilson?" Gilfillan asked, looking out the window at the elder Leeks scrambling over the log that functioned as a makeshift bridge. His voice had a distinctive Scots accent, but somewhere along the line it had been tempered by long exposure to the Queen's English.

Wilson's mind ran over all the mundane and supernatural things he had hunted while he changed. "No, not grouse, but I'm not new to hunting. I've gone deer and turkey hunting and done a lot of spear fishing, but that's not really the same thing, is it?"

Gilfillan popped up with a balled up pair of socks Wilson's size and chuckled, "No, not really."

"You won't find Gilfie within a hundred yards of the water line, Mr. Wilson," Ferris said without looking up from his phone. "Not since he saw *Jaws* as a kid and decided to heed the warning: 'Get out of the water!'"

"Quite a feat when you live on an island," Wilson drily commented.

"No sharks on land." The gamekeeper took the ribbing in stride as he searched for a pair of boots.

"If it's any consolation, I can attest that great whites are scarier in person than on screen," Wilson obliquely gave credence to the gamekeeper's shark-avoidance strategy.

"I'll gladly take your word for it," Gilfillan replied offhand as he handed Wilson the last of his kit: size-eight Wellington boots. "Parts of the moor are rather boggy," he explained, "and we had nearly a half inch of rain last night, so it's going to be wet out there once we get out of the near butt."

Wilson nodded and tried them on. "Fits perfectly."

"All right, that's it then; let's gets Sarge out of the kennel and head south." Gilfillan put on his heavy jacket.

"Best not to leave Basil and Grant alone out there armed and with only each other for company," Ferris explained to Wilson. Gilfillan smiled but did not comment.

Sarge was a well-trained black lab that kept pace with the group as they passed through the trees and up a ten-foot rise. They were on the moor just in time for the sun to peek through the low-level cloud cover, flooding the rolling lands with crimson and vermilion. Gilfillan led the way, carrying an extra shotgun as he would function as the loader for Wilson and Ferris. They quickly exited the shrubs near the woods and approached a hunting butt.

Dug into the earth, the butt only opened in the back and provided a screen for the hunter—grouse were fast game birds that flew low over the heather and could change direction mid-flight in an instant. Inside were two single-legged hunting stools that Gilfillan had already jammed deeply into the earth: one in the front of the butt for the shooter and other well behind.

"Would you like to shoot first, Mr. Wilson?" Ferris asked as they approached.

"Certainly. Thank you," Wilson replied, settling into the

front seat.

Gilfillan stood behind him, extra shotgun ready. "The grouse tend to come from the east here and fly out southwest. I've set three markers—the rocks with the yellow crosses on them—at the twenty-five, forty-five, and sixty yards. As you're a new grouse hunter, I recommend staying within the forty-five yard marker. Mentally allot two cartridges for each bird. If you down one with your first shot, try for another of course, but don't expect better than two per bird. Also, if you get a long flight and unload twice, pass your weapon to me with your right arm like this," he showed Wilson a single economical movement, "and I'll exchange it for mine and reload. If you're lucky enough to get a six-shot flight, we'll exchange weapons again."

"Understood." Wilson replied.

"A few safety points. Keep your barrel between the two wooden stakes at the front of the butt. We don't want any friendly fire. Also, stay behind the bunker, even when you aren't shooting. If you get a hit, we'll send Sarge out and he'll retrieve the kill."

Wilson nodded and men fell into silence, waiting for their prey. A gentle breeze brushed up the curves of the moor and the light dimmed as the sun rose above the cloud line. Suddenly, a burst of grouse cleared the hill. Two shots rang out from another butt, but the game was still airborne—it was late in the season and these grouse were wily survivors.

Wilson waited until their flight passed the stake on the left before taking two shots. There was a thud as two birds fell. Gilfillan had the secondary shotgun ready, but Wilson didn't pass his spent weapon and lowered it after the birds cleared the right stake.

Gilfillan whistled and sent Sarge out to retrieve the kill. "You're fast on the trigger, Mr. Wilson. You could have easily gotten another two shots, maybe more. Why didn't you pass?"

"I would have if I had missed, but two out of two is good enough. Its bad luck to take more than you need," Wilson explained.

Gilfillan gave the short man an odd stare when Ferris's phone started ringing. The blaring tone broke the quiet of the moor, and Wilson could hear Grant complain it about scaring away the game from the other butt.

Ferris sheepishly fished it out of his coat and was puzzled when he saw the caller ID. "Hello?" he answered. His face darkened and he suddenly became very serious. "Right. We'll leave immediately." There was more garbled noise on the other end. "Okay, I'll tell him," he said before hanging up.

"We have to go. Grandmother's had a heart attack. She's at York Hospital," Ferris announced. Gilfillan moved into action, letting Basil and Grant know and wrapping up the shoot. "Mr. Wilson," Ferris said timidly. "Father thinks it would be best if you found other accommodations considering the circumstances. It's a time for the family—just the family—to rally round."

Chapter Twelve

M62, Manchester, UK
4th of December, 10:35 a.m. (GMT)

Wilson engaged his clutch and up-shifted, weaving his car through the traffic between Leeds and Manchester, replaying the series of events that led to him being unceremoniously run out of Buttercrambe Hall. With Cordelia in ill health, Marmaduke was lord of the manor, and Wilson knew he was never in favor of calling the Salt Mine in the first place.

It had been a tense and silent ride back from the moors—not even Grant spoke. Wilson had been dropped off at the grand porte-cochère at the back of the house while the rest of the hunting party immediately headed out for the hospital. His rental BMW was waiting for him in front of the house, complete with his luggage that had been packed by Taylor.

Thankfully, Wilson had the foresight last night to return his gun to the secret compartment and load the visible sections to disguise any suspicious weight differential. He left word with the faithful butler that he would investigate elsewhere for a few days and return when Lady Leek recovered or her son requested his presence. Taylor promised to convey the message.

It wasn't rare for women in their sixties to have heart attacks, especially after a stressful event like the unexpected death of a grandchild, but the timing was suspicious—just a month after Asher's death and within twenty-four hours of Wilson's arrival at Buttercrambe Hall. There was always the possibility that Cordelia's karma had caught up with her—how much magic had she expended investigating Asher's death in the past month? Had she offset the cost with enough increased philanthropy? The Salt Mine had long ago derived mathematical equations to approximate karmic cost, but that knowledge was built with lots of data from hundreds of agents over the course of decades.

Assuming it wasn't karma or happenstance—Wilson generally didn't believe in coincidence in his line of work—it begged the question: were the Leeks were being targeted? If so, how were the other two deaths connected—practice for Asher's murder? Collateral damage?

The Mine hadn't found any link between the two other victims and Asher, other than they were all university students in Northern England. They were from different social classes, studied different subjects, and went to different universities. The trail had grown so cold on those cases that his best bet was to salvage what he could from Asher's demise.

One thing was for certain: he wasn't going to get voluntary access to Cordelia or the familial estate until her health improved. He knew he had nothing to do with her coronary event, but appearances were everything. So he found himself going to the only lead he could think of: Asher and Ferris's flat in Manchester. The address was included in his briefing, and Ferris was unlikely to return anytime soon with his grandmother in the hospital.

The flat was in the Northern Quarter of Manchester, a section of the city center between Piccadilly Station, Victoria Station, and Ancoats. Even though Manchester dated back to medieval times, the northern area wasn't developed until the late 1700s. Hosting a number of trades and industries over the years, it fell into disuse and disrepair in the twentieth century until it was repurposed and rebranded the "Northern Quarter" in the mid-1990s as an alternative residential area with a bohemian vibe.

Hailed a success of gentrification, the area was full of quirky, independent stores, cafes, bars, artists, and music—in short, the perfect place to be young, especially if your family could afford to buy a flat for you there. For the younger Durand Leek brother, it was very close to the University of Manchester, particularly the School of Mechanical, Aerospace, and Civil Engineering, and the Joule Library.

Wilson circled the block twice before finding a parking space, and the streets were packed with people minding their business and getting on with their day. He would have preferred to do this at night with ample time to do reconnaissance and plan, but he settled for a pass by of the building on foot. The security was minimal, no external cameras covering the exterior except for the front door buzzer system, and no wards were found. Most of the residents should be out: working, going to class, studying, running errands, or catching a late breakfast or early lunch.

He stopped by a flower shop and picked up a full bouquet that covered most of his face and returned to the stoop. He pressed the button for Ferris's flat, just to make sure it was empty. According to the files, no one else was registered to the address except for Ferris Leek, but the vagaries of youth were constantly in flux and rarely kept on top of administrative paperwork. When no one answered, he spoke into the intercom anyway and inserted a little thread of his will into the lock. He felt the tumblers roll into place with gentle pressure. The heavy front door opened, and any passersby wondered what lucky person was getting such a gorgeous arrangement.

Once he was inside, he bypassed the elevator and took the stairs to the fifth floor. The flat in question was a corner unit with an entrance close to the stairwell and tucked around the corner of the main hall. He checked Ferris's threshold for magical protections and found the enchanted evergreen wreath with bright red berries a mild deterrent that was easily bypassed. When he was certain the hallway was clear, he pulled out his lock picks and opened the door the old-fashioned way—no need to use magic unless required.

Tastefully furnished with a modern aesthetic, the flat was a vast departure from Buttercrambe Hall. It was bright, with sparse furniture, clean lines, and lots of chrome and glass. The only antique in plain sight was a mid-century foosball table, or table football as the Brits would call it. Mounted on the living room wall was the larger version of the television in Asher's dressing room and the games and controllers were not nearly as tidy. The kitchen was packed with high-end appliances that were mostly holding beer and frozen foods. There was no designated dining area except for the coffee table and couch, or the barstools against the kitchen counter.

It wasn't hard to tell which room belonged to which brother, given the disparity in their interests. Asher's was filled with history books and Dr. Who paraphernalia and Ferris's with engineering and Star Trek. Wilson didn't waste time and salted the apartment. It was large by UK standards but a shoebox compared to the 500.

Unlike his suites in Buttercrambe Hall, Asher's room looked lived in and untouched. His bed was unmade, there were clothes strewn about, and the top of his desk was cluttered with notes, books, pens, highlighters, and other office knickknacks, including a Tardis pencil holder. There definitely wasn't a cleaner visiting regularly, mundane or supernatural.

As Wilson had suspected, Asher's signature shook out crisp and clear. He snapped a picture with his phone and checked the rest of the room. His thoroughness was rewarded when he found another magical signature tucked in the back of Asher's closet. It was faint and fuzzy, like a memory of magic, but it was definitely not Leek in composition. Wilson shined a light on it and took a picture for the Mine to identify.

Wilson's eye traced a rectangular outline in the dust on the bottom of the closet—whatever was there, it wasn't there anymore. He pulled out the hag stone and did a sweep. *One… two…three…* Nothing. On a hunch, he tried Ferris's room. Taylor seemed willing to cover for Asher; why not his brother?

Ferris was more fastidious than his older brother. He actually used a linen hamper and wastebasket, and the amount of ambient body spray still lingering in the air suggested he was concerned with the appearance of personal hygiene. There was a place for everything, which made searching easier. Stashed on the top shelf, shoved behind an empty gym bag, was a box roughly the same size as the silhouette in Asher's closet.

Wilson opened it and found the normal assortment of items no one wants their parents to see: condoms, drugs, and anything remotely kinky. There were more over-the-counter pills and underneath it all, he found evidence of ritual magic: chalk, a perfectly circular silvered mirror, tea light candles, and incense. Someone was doing some divination, and it wasn't Ferris.

He picked up a small notebook, hoping Asher kept a diary of some sort since all his notes for his dissertation were at his desk. Unfortunately, it was just lists of topics, and it wasn't limited to history. Wilson recognized names of physicists, mathematical principles, notes about geography, chemical elements, names of authors and their works, references to pieces of art and music. They were all jumbled together in no discernable order, but by each entry was a pair of letters: AL, DW, DB, or GW.

As he flipped through the pages of tight scrawl, he saw a pattern start to form: all the mathematics and physics question had DB next to them, all the history questions AL, the music and art questions GW.... Something clicked in his head and he laughed at loud in disbelief—Asher was divining to cheat on Bletchley Park Challenge and punting the topics to the right team member so it wouldn't look suspicious when they kept getting answers right. *Driven young man, indeed.* He sighed as he put the notebook down.

Wilson took out the hag stone and gave the contents a once over, and his heart skipped a beat—the sheet of pills lit up. He pulled the stone away from his eye and ran his will over them. Then he carefully picked them up with his gloved hand and placed it on the floor. Using his saltcaster, he waited for the fine grains to form a pattern: a cleaner version of what he'd found in Asher's closet. Wilson flipped the packet and read the fine print on the back: Caffeine, 200 mg.

Chapter Thirteen

Detroit, Michigan, USA
4th of December, 6:25 a.m. (GMT-5)

Emmitt Parson's eyes flickered over his three monitors: the first on the CIA, the second on the FBI, and the third a collation of the excised essentials that would make up today's briefing. His long fingers danced across the keyboard as he rapidly typed a message and sent the document to the appropriate department for dissemination. By the end of the hour, it would be sitting in every Salt Mine agent's in-basket, either on their phone or in their office in a battered manila folder with OFFICIAL – SM EYES ONLY inked in black.

A familiar blur came over his vision, and he closed his eyes and counted to ten slowly. His ophthalmologist assured him his current prescription and eyes were fine—he just needed to blink more. Apparently, it was a common problem among people who worked in front of computers and screens all day, especially if it required deep focus. He felt stupid doing blink exercises, but it was a cheaper and easier fix than eye drops.

Parson lived in an electronic world, combing through the web for connections. The fractious nature of information made his job more challenging, but it made the discoveries all the more rewarding. He'd developed a gut instinct about these things over the years, what some might call a sixth sense, but he liked to think of it as a highly developed observational judgment. He knew something was fishy before his brain could find reason in it, much less elucidate with words. It was like those nurses and doctors who knew something was wrong with a patient even though they were fine by the numbers. Thankfully, he didn't have to know the whys; he just had to flag the information and send it up the pipeline.

Parson liked working nights because the stream of data was coming in from other parts of the world that were up and active while the US slept. He had his very own front-row seat to the world in the comfort of his ergonomic office chair. He hadn't traveled much—too much hassle and it usually required flying, which was a deal breaker. Just the thought of being trapped in a metal tube between 31,000 and 38,000 feet in the air made him break out in a cold sweat. The fact that it was an aerodynamic tube did little to ease his jitters.

His shift would be over soon, and it had been a productive day. His official position was Data Analyst at Discretion Minerals, and the cover title made his work seem more glamorous—one step closer to wearing tuxedos and drinking martinis shaken, not stirred.

He'd been assigned as lead researcher to the Leek investigation and spent much of the early evening transcribing conversations picked up by the bugs and when possible, identifying speakers and where the conversations were taking place in from a possible list of rooms. It was like a fusion of Clue and Guess Who, except he wasn't allowed to ask any questions to further his work. The people were letters and the rooms numbers at the start of the night, and a self-satisfied smile crossed his face each time a variable became known. The house had been quiet since Cordelia Leek was taken to the hospital, and he knocked out the dailies to give the new analyst a break. Once upon a time, he was the new kid on the block.

With no outstanding requests from agents on specific searches, Parson dove into the sea of ones and zeros, letting them wash over him until he found something significant. There was always a standing list of things to be alert to, and analysts were often the first to pick up patterns in the ever-chaotic swell of big data.

Something sparked his interest on the middle screen: Jennifer Drake, twenty-six-year-old student at the University of Bedfordshire, was lying in cold storage in Milton Keynes University Hospital, awaiting autopsy. He pulled up a map of the UK on the left screen; Ms. Drake was a university student with what was deemed a suspicious death, but her school wasn't in the north. Milton Keynes was some hundred and twenty miles south of the cluster of northern universities attended by the three dead students previously flagged, but it was only a few miles from where Asher Leek had died. Plus, Parson's gut was yelling at him.

Parson moved his mouse and started typing, sneaking in through the backdoor he'd set up on a previous hack. He scanned for details on the deceased and smiled. *Bingo.* He flagged the file "Urgent" and sent it up for immediate review.

*****

Leader balanced the coffee carrier and sack of croissants in one hand as she presented her eye and palm to the elevator scanner. Once it took, she pressed level six for her weekly breakfast with the twins. She knew it was good for her to get out of her office for a social call, but the realities of the job didn't make it easy. Her compromise was to breakfast with Chloe and Dot, since going to the sixth floor didn't involve going through security like catching coffee or a meal topside would.

"We're going Parisian—chocolate croissants," she announced as she approached the circular desk at the end of the stacks.

"Where did you get them?" Dot asked suspiciously as Leader put everything on the desk far from any books.

She cocked one eyebrow and almost smiled. "Does it really matter? It's a croissant stuffed with chocolate."

"Don't mind her," Chloe addressed Leader as she claimed a cup from the four-pack carrier and popped the lid to put in sugar and creamer. "She's just mad she drew the short stick this morning."

"Oh?" the salt-and-pepper-haired woman intoned innocently and sipped her black coffee. "Whatcha working on?"

Dot took the last coffee and smirked while Chloe chided Leader, "Nothing that can't wait thirty minutes," she sidestepped the question as she took out a flaky pastry from the bag. "This is girls breakfast. We should be talking about the latest thing you've made or a great book you've read—"

"Or a piece of ass you're tapped," Dot interrupted mischievously. Chloe elbowed her sister and Dot nudged her back. "You might as well tell her. It's going to drive her crazy until you do." Leader scowled at her, who—in true Dot fashion—was helping in the most insulting way possible. "These *are* good," the surly blonde added before taking another bite.

"I'm so glad you approve," Leader feigned relief and took the last from the sack. "So, read any good books lately?" She tried to a little too hard to sound buoyant, and Chloe cringed inside at her attempt at small talk. Leader was a serious person who talked about serious things; frivolity didn't suit her, but bless her heart, she was trying.

A wave of mercy came over Dot as she swallowed another buttery morsel. "Wilson found another magical signature at Asher Leek's Manchester apartment—on over-the-counter caffeine pills, of all things."

"Caffeine pills?" Leader said incredulously. "Points for creativity."

"It may have nothing to do with his death," Dot qualified the discovery. "Asher had the same brand of pills at Buttercrambe Hall but they weren't enchanted."

"Still, it's something," Leader said hopefully as she chewed through her breakfast and the new intel.

Chloe sighed and gave up on trying to have a work-free girls breakfast. "He's going to overnight the pills to the Mine, so we can't do any testing just yet, but we have a hit on the signature." She brushed off the crumbs and wiped her hands before retrieving a file. "Shyam Bhatt, PhD, professor of History at University of Leeds."

"Signature picked up during a convention of practitioners in Salem, Massachusetts ten years ago, but no trouble on file," Dot added.

"And before you ask, we've already sent the name to the analysts for a bio and any connection to the other university students who have died," Chloe took the baton. "So you don't have to worry. We've got it under control. Now, tell us how Thanksgiving went. How was Chuck?"

"Old, Korean, and cranky," Leader joked between bites.

"So same old, same old," Dot jabbed.

"But he didn't say 'no' right off the bat?" Chloe said with amazement. "That's promising."

A ripple of energy broke the intimate gathering, and suddenly a silky black cat appeared on the desk with a can of tuna in her mouth. "Hello, Mau," Leader greeted the unexpected visitor.

The cat dropped the metal disk on the table at the sound of her real name and gingerly nudged it forward with her paw. "Can you open?" she asked in a raspy voice. "Crawling Shadow is gone and the Mountain wasn't home."

Dot saw the wounds on her paw and gasped. "What happened, kitty?"

"Porcupine," Mau answered tersely but she lapped up the concern and affection. "I ate it." She flicked her tail victoriously.

Chloe pulled some rubbing alcohol and cotton balls from one of the numerous drawers of their circular desk. She didn't know if mummy cats got infections, but best not chance it. "Did you like it?" she inquired as she applied first aid. It had been so long since she'd eaten porcupine that she didn't remember what it tasted like, only that she and Dot didn't care for it.

"I wouldn't eat another except to spite it," Mau answered honestly. "Open?"

"Certainly," Leader answered and took it in hand. "Chloe, do you have a plate? We can't have her eating out of the can." She caught the ring on the top with her fingernail and pulled the top off. Mau purred at the fishy smell. Leader spooned the tuna out, breaking up the big chunks into flakes, and distributed the juice evenly. Only then did she present the plate to Mau, who graciously accepted it.

They set work aside and switched to benign topics while Mau ate, and after she was finished, they took turns doting on her. Chloe was amazed at the change in Leader's demeanor; she was almost relaxed and sociable. Her gaze was still keen, but less intense while she made blithe remarks about something of absolutely no consequence. Mau was stretched on her back in Leader's lap and got her belly rubbed.

Chloe saw the change in Leader's eyes before she spoke. "Mau, Wilson has something important that he needs to give us. If we let him know you were coming first, do you think you could pick it up from him and bring it here?"

Mau rolled to her paws and onto the desk where she could sit level with Leader. Her emerald eyes met Leader's steely gray pupils, reading the merit of the request. She tossed her head toward the empty pastry sack. "You bring one for Mau next time?"

"Chocolate and croissants aren't good for cats," Leader played hardball, "but I will bring a special treat just for you."

It was a mental game of catch the mouse, and Mau did love a worthy opponent. "Bring two," she negotiated.

"Deal," Leader coolly replied. "Let me call and make sure he hasn't already sent it." Mau smiled and nodded. The Faithful One was always good to her word.

Chapter Fourteen

Milton Keynes, Buckinghamshire, UK
4th of December, 2:45 p.m. (GMT)

DCI Simon Jones entered through the main entrance of Milton Keynes University Hospital, one of facilities that housed the dead for the Thames Valley Police when a suspicious death called for an autopsy. He didn't need to ask for directions or consult the map on the wall; he was well acquainted with the path to the morgue. He put his hand under the hand sanitizer dispenser and rubbed the cold goo liberally over his hands before proceeding.

Unlike the other hospitals that were a single multi-storied building with outlying additions, Milton Keynes University Hospital was a sprawling mass of low-lying buildings linked by endless corridors. Numerous green areas were tucked in between sections, so getting around required more ambulation than more traditional construction. It must have been nice for the patients but it was a nuisance for Jones. After what felt like *at least* half a kilometer, he descended into the basement occupied by the morgue.

He presented his identification to the guard who was

expecting him and walked down a long and distressingly dim hallway. He paused outside the off-white swinging doors and almost talked himself into waiting there for his 3:00 p.m. appointment with Agent Wilson of Interpol. He checked his watch as he vacillated, but eventually he decided it would be more awkward not to enter.

Jones didn't care for morgues. Intellectually, he knew they were a necessary part of his job, but they gave him the willies. He'd seen plenty of terrible things as a homicide detective but never felt the slightest tremor while performing his job in the field. He'd been disgusted and even vomited once at a particularly bad scene, but he was never nervous or faint. But the instant he was confronted by an autopsy, he always had to consciously work to keep his cool. It wasn't the blood and gore that bothered him; no, it was quite the opposite. He found the clinical nature of an autopsy disturbing.

If he walked onto a crime scene and found a person's brains bashed in or guts spilling out of a knife wound, that was clearly wrong. Someone had taken away a person's life—their very humanity—and he was going to find them and bring them to justice. But cutting open bodies, taking out organs, and weighing them methodically in a sterile room? He found that infinitely creepier because that was standard operating procedure.

He gathered his fortitude for whatever was on the other side of the doors and pushed through. On the slab was the body of Jennifer Drake, who was a living, breathing young women yesterday. She was months away from graduating from university and had her whole life ahead of her. Now, her corpse was split open with her internal organs in their own small stainless steel containers placed on the adjacent table. Each had been weighed and sampled, waiting to be rejoined with Drake's body once the medical examiner was finished with them.

Dr. Akuma Boateng, the local medical examiner, looked up from her work and her sapphire studs caught the light just right to sparkle. "Good afternoon, DCI Jones. You're just in time for the big reveal," she greeted him. Even though she was wearing a face mask, he could tell by the mirth in her big brown eyes that she was having a laugh at him.

"Don't mind me," he said as he raised a hand and excused himself to a far corner. Boateng made a practiced cut behind one of Drake's ears and traveled the scalpel's blade over the top of her head to end at the same place behind her other ear. Placing the blade down, the ME grabbed the flap of skin she'd released from Drake's scalp and pulled the front flap of the scalp forward, revealing the glistening skull beneath. It sounded like the rind of a cantaloupe being pulled apart. She then did the same for the back half.

Jones steadied himself as Boateng reached for the rotary bone saw—he knew what was coming next. He heard the hum of the motor and the tone of the reverberation change as the blade made contact with bone. He looked away and gave himself a pep talk. *You haven't fainted since you were a cadet, Jonesy; let's keep that record intact.*

The ME's expertise made quick work of Drake's skull and had the deceased's brain removed and in its own pan. "Patient's brain weighs one one five seven grams," Boateng stated for the recording; there was no hint of emotion in her voice.

Better her than I, Jones thought, as he breathed in through his nose and out of his mouth. He wasn't wired to perform dispassionate desecration of a body, even in the name of science and justice. "Is that normal?" he asked after he recovered.

"No, that's far underweight. For a young woman, it should be around 1350 grams," she replied as she removed the brain from the scale and carried it to her dissection table. The various tools of her trade gleamed on the mayo stand. "Where's your guest?"

"Agent Wilson? He was supposed to meet me here at three," he answered.

Boateng looked at the clock: 15:03. "I've never worked with Interpol before," the doctor said as she picked up a scalpel in her gloved hand.

"I worked with him once, about a year ago. Serious gent. Focused," Jones summarized his impressions from their brief interaction in the Grollo case last year.

"Birds of a feather?" Boateng commented without looking up. "If you don't mind me asking, why's Interpol getting involved?"

Jones hesitated briefly but saw little benefit in being a stickler for the rules. As much as he couldn't fathom doing her job, he knew her to be a professional, and she would conduct a thorough autopsy regardless. "Apparently there have been a few other cases in Eastern Europe. Ukraine, Belarus, etc."

"And they believe there's a drug connection?" Boateng guessed based on the full toxicology request that had just landed on her desk. They always screened for the usual suspects and took more blood and urine samples in case further testing for metabolites were required to pin down the illicit drug in question.

"You'd have to ask Agent Wilson about that," Jones stated neutrally. "I'm just the guy showing him around while he's in town."

"And you bring him to the morgue? Remind me never to hire you as a tour guide," she teased him.

The morgue doors swung open a millisecond before Wilson entered. "My apologies for being late, DCI Jones. There was an accident on the highway and I had to take smaller roads."

Jones shook the proffered hand and noted Wilson's thinness under the well-fitted suit. "No worries, Agent Wilson. It's good to see you again, although I dare say there is significantly less of you to see."

"I started a new diet and exercise regimen recently," Wilson vaguely answered, as if it was intentional.

"Maybe you can share your secret with the good DCI,"

Boateng commented with one hand on Drake's brain and the other on the gliding scalpel.

"And that is Dr. Boateng," Jones introduced the ME, who nodded at Wilson since her hands were otherwise unavailable to shake.

She finished her cut and took a good look at the inside of Drake's brain, poking and prodding with her surgical tools. Her demeanor shifted and all levity in her face and tone disappeared. "If I didn't know better, I'd swear this wasn't the brain of a twenty-six-year-old."

Wilson grabbed a pair of gloves and a face mask from the box mounted on the wall and moved toward the corpse without hesitation. Jones reluctantly followed. Dr. Boateng used the end of her probe as a pointer, tracing the hollows in the middle of the brain. "These are ventricles. They contain cerebrospinal fluid, the stuff that brings in nutrients and takes out waste," she simplified the anatomy for her audience. "They are always present in healthy brains, but these are twice as big as they should be. And that's not the only thing that's weird. See here?" She pointed to the exterior of the brain. "The ridges and grooves on the surface are smaller than normal and the gray matter is thinner than it should be on cross-section. Even the dimensions of the brain are well below average."

"If you were looking at this brain without context, what sort of conclusions would you draw?" Wilson asked.

"Honestly, a geriatric person with chronic normal pressure

hydrocephalus, possibly dementia, depending on their clinical presentation before death," Boateng answered, befuddled. "But it doesn't make sense in a twenty-six-year-old woman. A traumatic brain injury or serious infection that caused swelling of the brain would explain the increased ventricle size, but not the shrinking of the brain."

She turned to Wilson. "And you say there are more young people with this presentation on autopsy?"

"I'm not at liberty to discuss ongoing investigations, but Interpol is committed to facilitating collaboration between agencies to get to the bottom of this," Wilson parroted a believable line of jargon. "When will all the testing results be available?"

"Realistically, forty-eight hours. Maybe sooner if I press," she replied tersely; Wilson's officious answer ran against her grain.

"If you would, that'll be great," Wilson kept up his off-putting tone. If she was annoyed with him, she wasn't asking inconvenient questions.

Dr. Boateng didn't look up from her work. "Then consider it done. Now, if you gentlemen would leave me to it…"

"Certainly! Thank you for your time, Dr Boateng," Jones replied and politely ushered Wilson out with him. He hoped he'd acted fast enough to salvage his good rapport with the ME.

They walked in silence through the basement until they reached daylight again and Jones tested the waters. "So you think this is drug related?"

Wilson gave a weary smile. "I'm just the guy collecting information on the ground so the much smarter people can do their job. Right now, Interpol is just trying to gather all the information we can regarding the cases here and in Eastern Europe, and see if there's any obvious connections."

"We just found Jennifer Drake this morning—that's some fast reaction time on Interpol's part," Jones gave a measured opinion.

Wilson smirked at the implication. "The rather public nature of Asher Leek's death brought the possible cases in the UK to our attention," he offered a plausible explanation. "Ms. Drake's untimely demise was an unfortunate coincidence, but it could help shed more light if there is a connection."

Jones's face lit up in comprehension and sympathy. When Asher Leek had died, his entire force was put on the case, and there had been a lot of pressure from his superiors for a quick solution. When a vocal and influential family like the Leeks yanks on the right chains, Bob's your uncle. *Looks like the Leeks pulled far and wide*, Jones thought to himself. "It was an unsettling death," Jones spoke with authority.

"I understand you were there?" Wilson asked casually.

Jones nodded. "Night out as a treat from my wife," he said with a little sadness. "He didn't go peacefully—spent his last minutes shaking and his last breaths yelling."

The DCI shook the memory from his head and changed

the subject. "So what happened to the Grollo case you were pursuing the last time you were here? I didn't hear anything about it after Dr. Brinston ruled it a suicide." His stress on the last word emphasized how little faith he had in it.

Wilson had formulated his response on the drive over from Manchester. "That? It ended being some sort of heavy metal poisoning—a case of accidental exposure at some posh charity dinner. You weren't filled in?" He played his part with affected surprise to perfection.

"No, I was not," Jones sighed as he opened the front door to the hospital.

Wilson gave a short, well-rehearsed laugh. "Figures. They have all the resources in the world to get new chairs at the Lyon HQ, but they don't have enough staff to send out mission summations when a case has been closed. Makes you wonder whose warming all those seats?"

Jones's collegial snort was all the confirmation Wilson needed—cover story sold. "I *knew* Grollo didn't kill himself," Jones muttered as he opened the doors to his car.

"Well, he *did* eat the paintings," Wilson corrected him as he slid into the DCI's passenger seat. "But he wasn't in his right mind. Who knew poorly-manufactured, seventeenth-century Romanov chafing dishes were reactive with a modern cleaning agent?" Wilson added, tying the bow on the lie. It was a sublime mix of specificity and ridiculousness that smacked of the truth; a liar would choose something more generic and vague.

"Ready to see Drake's flat?" Jones asked as he turned the engine over.

"Only if you've cleared the scene; I don't want to get in the way," Wilson said obligingly.

Jones glanced at the time in his car and reached for his phone. "DC Tull should have everything wrapped up by now. Let me give him a ring to make sure that everything's clear before we head over."

Chapter Fifteen

Milton Keynes, Buckinghamshire, UK
4th of December, 3:45 p.m. (GMT)

The town of Milton Keynes was a modern invention, established in the 1960s. Designed to house a quarter of a million people, it was the largest of similar towns created in southeast England to alleviate the housing congestion in London. At the time, the area was sparsely inhabited and the village of Milton Keynes was expanded to incorporate existing towns in the area, including Bletchley, Wolverton, and Stony Stratford, as well as fifteen other villages and the farmland in between.

While some objected to forced urbanization, others lauded the injection in population and resources to the area. Unlike places that modernized piecemeal with pre-existing infrastructure, Milton Keynes had the opportunity to build with a larger vision from the beginning and sidestep the pitfalls that organic growth had created for other towns and cities. They could have their multiplex cinemas, theaters, galleries, concert halls, universities, and teaching hospitals without compromising their rustic charm or choking on automobile congestion.

The planners retained and showcased Milton Keynes's historic buildings: the thatched roof pub, village hall, church, and surviving traditional homes. They protected the linear parks that ran through the town's designated acreage, keeping the landscape for flood management while providing the residents plenty of parkland and lakeside scenery.

The tall new sleek modern facilities were built in the central business district, but outside of that area, residential structures were limited to a height of three stories. There would be no monolithic tower blocks for Milton Keynes. The planners relaxed the grid of distributor roads to avoid the traffic jams endemic to other urbanized areas, and paths for pedestrians and cyclists crisscrossed the town to promote non-vehicular travel. It was only fifty miles from London, but it seemed worlds apart.

Wilson wasn't able to appreciate the landscape on his frantic drive to the hospital—he hated being late—but he was taking it all in from the passenger seat of DCI Jones's car. It was quite a departure from the moors he was in earlier today. During the drive, Jones laid out what they knew so far about the case, and Wilson nodded every so often to show he was listening.

Jennifer Drake was working at a local primary school as an unqualified teacher while pursuing her bachelor's degree in Applied Education Studies at the University of Bedfordshire.

She was found dead in her room this morning by her roommate, Lauren Wilkinson. There were no signs of an altercation in her room, assault on her body, or a suicide note. There was no one else in the flat last night except for the two women who lived there. Both Drake and Wilkinson had no criminal records, with the exception of the occasional speeding ticket.

They parked next to a quaint building and walked up the stairs to the third floor. Remnants of police tape were still in place; the only evidence remaining of the bevy of morning activity. Jones knocked on the front door while Wilson stood behind, running his will over the entrance. There were no wards in place.

A shaken young woman answered the door. "Lauren, this is Agent Wilson from Interpol. He would like to take a look around and ask you a few questions, if now is a convenient time." Wilson extended his hand and she limply accepted it.

Her ponytail bobbed as she nodded her head and let them in. "I really don't know what else I could tell you. I already told DC Tull everything I know."

"Why don't you start by telling Agent Wilson what happened this morning," Jones suggested gently.

She plopped herself on the couch and curled her feet under her. "This morning, I slept in because I didn't have class until 9:00, and when I left my room, I saw Jennifer's stuff was still here—which was weird because she works during the day and goes to class at night. I knocked on her bedroom door. When she didn't answer, I opened it to take a peek and make sure she was okay. That's when I found her." She paused to stifle tears, and Jones offered her a box of tissues sitting on the side table. She brushed him aside and continued. "I knew something wasn't right. Her eyes were open but she wasn't there."

"What sort of things was she involved with outside of work and school?" Wilson asked.

"She didn't have time for anything else," Wilkinson asserted. "If she wasn't working, she was in class or studying in her room. I don't even think she's been on a date since I moved in last year. She kept to herself, did her fair share of the housework, and didn't eat my food. Except for the smelly incense she burned from time to time, she was pretty much the perfect roommate."

Wilson perked up. "Incense?"

"Yeah, she was a pagan; called herself a druidess. Every month, she would walk around 'purifying the flat,'" she elaborated with a hint of sarcasm. Then, her brow furrowed as a thought came to her. "Was Jennifer into something I need to be worried about? I mean, *Interpol*?" Wilson saw her imagination start to go wild with convoluted plots. *It's always the quite ones.*

"We're just being thorough," he replied to slow her down, but she looked less than convinced. "Why? Was Jennifer acting strange recently or have any other peculiar habits?"

Wilkinson shook her head. "No, but we weren't exactly best friends."

"Did she use any drugs?" he asked.

"You're kidding?" Wilkinson scoffed. "She was so uptight about that kind of stuff when I asked about the room. I don't think she even smoked pot. Now a glass of wine at the end of the day…"

Wilson pointed to the narrow hallway opposite the small kitchen. "Her room was down the hall?"

"Yeah, she had the one in the back with all the crap on the door. She was supposed to repaint it and the frame before we moved so we could get the security deposit back." Wilson saw the cracks in the facade before Jones and made for the hallway before the tears started. "I'm so sorry," she apologized. "This keeps happening. We weren't even that close."

Wilson and Jones exchanged looks across the room and came to a tacit agreement. "I think we're almost done here," Jones consoled the distraught young woman as Wilson moved to examine Drake's room. "Is there someone you can call to stay here with you? Or maybe you have somewhere else you can stay for a few days until Jennifer's family clears out her things?"

The conversation that followed became an indistinct muffle as Wilson approached the bedroom door. There was a motley collection of runes and sigils from various cultures and disciplines, all drawn in permanent marker. He brushed his will across the surface—*think…think…think*—and found arcane power behind them. The wards were simplistic and they melted away with just a nudge of Wilson's will, bending the black markings slightly out-of-line and rendering them impotent.

The room inside was economic but functional: a narrow unmade bed, a wooden study table with a plastic rolling chair, a bookshelf with a few dozen books, and a cheap, self-assembly wardrobe that was mostly particle board. The walls were bare except for a single poster for a band he'd never heard of and a large whiteboard with signs of heavy use.

He listened at the doorway and heard more talking, rummaging in the kitchen, and the click of the electric kettle. All signs suggested the DCI was preoccupied with Wilkinson making a cuppa—the English balm against all aliments, especially moral injury.

Wilson closed the door behind him and blew the fine grains from his saltcaster onto the cheap laminate flooring. He performed a quick perusal of the spines while he waited and found a healthy selection of pagan and occult books, all of them of the mass-produced variety. A random spot check revealed no liner notes. *Useless drivel*, Wilson thought as he returned the titles to where he'd found them.

When he looked back to the floor, the salt had divided into two separate patterns. The one in front of the white board was new to him, but he recognized the one at Drake's desk—it was the same one he'd found at Asher's apartment. Wilson hurriedly took pictures, kicked the salt, and pulled out the hag stone. *One…two…three…* The white board lit up with layer upon layer of sigils and circles—clearly, where Drake had been practicing her craft. It was the final piece of evidence Wilson needed to confirm his suspicions: Jennifer Drake was a magician of sorts, but one untutored and/or new to magic. Practice should occur in materials that mattered, like chalk, charcoal, iron, silver, gold, salt, or blood—not dry erase or permanent marker.

Four…five…six… Wilson moved objects around on the top of the desk and opened drawers, looking for the source of the second magical signature. A bright spot filled the washed-out contents of the drawer: a packet of caffeine pills.

He extracted the pack and deposited them in his pocket along with the hag stone when he heard footsteps and voices approaching. The color returned to the room and Wilson resumed his search to keep up appearances. DCI Jones opened the door to Wilson mundanely searching Drake's desk. "Ms. Wilkinson is gathering a few things to stay at a friend's place for a few days, but I've got her contact information should you have further questions for her."

Wilson closed the drawer and sighed heavily. "Thank you, but I think I've got everything I need from here."

"Nothing of interest?" Jones asked.

"Not unless you want to read about the latest theories of pedagogy for students on the spectrum, or druidess spells," Wilson drily remarked.

Jones smirked and nodded. “I’ll give you a lift back to your car at the hospital.”

Chapter Sixteen

Leeds, Yorkshire, UK
4th of December, 9:45 p.m. (GMT)

The kid manning the cash register looked up from his phone when Wilson entered the convenience store and triggered the electronic door chime. Once he'd recognized Wilson as a customer, evidenced by the cut of his bespoke suit under the raincoat, instead of one of the local bums, he returned to his flash game. Only fifteen minutes before his shift was up, and then the store was someone else's problem.

Wilson gave his umbrella a good shake outside before collapsing it and picking up a shopping basket. The soles of his shoes squeaked on the linoleum floor as he walked up and down the aisles and took stock of the store. He'd deliberately picked it because of its proximity to the University of Leeds, and it looked much the same as the other stores he'd visited since he'd left Jennifer Drake's apartment. It had essentials in modest quantities for students ever short on cash and space: small quantities of toiletries, loo rolls by the single or four pack, candy and chips—Crisps, he corrected himself—premade foods in heated cases, and a selection of foodstuffs that only required a kettle, toaster, or microwave to "cook." A small corner held school supplies, and the long wall held a vast array of sodas and energy drinks.

Then, there was the shelves of nutraceuticals and medications sold over-the-counter. Anyone over sixteen could buy food and drink containing caffeine without showing ID, and they certainly didn't have to go to a chemist for caffeine pills. They were sold right next to the vitamins.

By now, Wilson was well acquainted with what he was looking for. He cherry-picked four boxes of caffeine pills and headed to the counter. He paid cash for his purchase and stuffed the receipt in the bag with the tablets. With his package tucked under his coat, he took shelter under the umbrella until he was back inside his rented BMW. The windows fogged up as the engine engaged. Wilson shifted the heat to the defrost setting and added the paper bag to the growing stack on the passenger side floorboard. Once he regained visibility of his rearview and side mirrors, he headed back to his hotel room.

Wilson had settled on staying in Leeds for a couple of reasons. First, he wanted to be close to Buttercrambe Hall in case Marmaduke Leek had a change of heart. Second, that was where Shyam Bhatt resided and worked. The analysts made quick work connecting the dots once the librarians supplied them a name. While Dr. Bhatt was a tenured professor at the University of Leeds, he'd attended a conference on Asian Studies hosted by the University of Liverpool in late August, and a credit card receipt put him in Milton Keynes three weeks ago.

After conducting some forensic magic on the pills found at Asher's Manchester flat, Chloe and Dot ruled out murder as the prime motivator, but the enchantment did targeted the neural pathways. Whatever the intent, using caffeine pills as the transmission vehicle was a deliberate and effective choice. Caffeine was a fast-acting stimulant that acted on the central nervous system, i.e. the brain. Using the same pathways and neurotransmitters as the fight-or-flight response, it increased the amount of energy metabolized by the brain while decreasing cerebral blood flow. Often used to help people stay awake, it was *the* most popular study supplement in students, as moderate doses helped focus due to the local release of dopamine in the brain.

Based on the number of boxes Wilson had in his car, there had to be way more affected students than the four dead ones. With confirmation that two out of the four dead were practitioners, Chloe and Dot's best guess was that magicians were particularly sensitive to the effects, something akin to a severe adverse effect that manifested as aggressive brain remodeling. The induced state of relative brain hypoperfusion from caffeine should have been transient since caffeine's half-life was only three to five hours, and anyone taking megadoses of caffeine was more likely to have anxiety, nausea and vomiting, profuse sweating, increased heart rate and respirations, and high blood pressure—not a seizure and an elderly person's brain on autopsy.

If it were up to Wilson, he would have simply put a bullet in Bhatt's head. With the source magician gone, wrapping up the case was simply a matter of finding and destroying all the enchanted pills that were already in circulation. If need be, he knew of a winged maker he could call upon to help round them up. However, Leader had other plans for Dr. Bhatt.

Her instructions had been clear: confront the magician with what they knew and recruit him as an asset. She knew there was no way the Dawn Club would ever let Bhatt into their circle—they were entirely too racist and he too brown for that—but the Mine needed contacts within in the UK's magical community however it could get them.

Wilson was just the agent for the job. He'd had plenty of experience recruiting oppositional assets, going back to his CIA days. He'd like to think his penchant for finding the right points of stress and leverage was part of the reason Leader gave him the codename Fulcrum.

Wilson had already driven by the professor's home and found it well warded, another confirmation that Bhatt was a competent caster, much more advanced than poor Jennifer Drake would ever become now. The sudden streak of sympathy and sadness had surprised Wilson; he'd long become inured with the cruel realities of life, both petty and substantial. But something about Drake's death bothered him deeply. She was an unqualified teacher, probably making less than £20,000 a year, who was a veritable infant in terms of practicing magic. She was just looking for a way to get more productive hours in the day, and for that, she died.

Wilson slinked into his hotel and suddenly understood why dogs felt the need to violently shake the water off when they got wet. He peeled off his clothes and toweled himself off as best he could. Once he was in warm, dry clothes, he hung up his wet items to dry by the radiator. He pulled out his phone and added "empathy for victims" to his list of changes.

He then opened the detailed instructions Chloe and Dot had sent him for destroying the pills. He'd collected twenty boxes in total from five different quick stores, all near universities. He didn't know how many more there were—and he'd be surprised if this was all of them—but it was twenty fewer floating out in the world.

He methodically gathered all the supplies and laid them out in the bathroom: latex gloves, a plastic bucket, a drinking glass, a measuring cup, a bottle of distilled water, baking soda, ammonia, and salt. Then, there was the incantation. Wilson recognized part of it from the seventeenth-century work *On Putrefaction and Ill Winds*. It contained a hymn used to purify "poisonous miasmas" and had saved a fair number of practitioners from a number of infectious diseases in a time when germs were unheard of. The other sections were integrating the other materials into the ritual. Thankfully, it was all in Latin, which was stronger than his Greek.

He read over the document three times to make sure he understood the order of operations. It reminded him of setting up an experiment in chemistry class on lab day. First, he gloved up and popped all the pills from their blister packs into the bucket. Next, he circled the bucket with salt. Then, he summoned his will and started his litany, temporarily enchanting the baking soda with purifying properties that would be used later in the hymn.

He put equal parts magical baking soda and ammonia in the glass and stirred with a clean spoon left over from his takeout. He timed each revolution with the exactly line and verse, per the twin's directions. Then he poured distilled water into the paste until it formed a loose solution.

Wilson could feel the power cumulate with each step, and when he finally poured the solution over the pills, he felt all that energy burst like a sonic boom that pushed out against the salt, but the circle held. He wondered what sort of damage it would have done uncontained. Nullified, all of the smelly, magically inert mess went into the toilet, and he watched it circle the drain over several flushes.

He plugged in his phone to charge the battery and tapped a message to the Mine. *20 boxes destroyed; tomorrow approach Bhatt.* Satisfied with the day's work, he climbed into bed and wrapped himself in the crisp, clean hotel sheets.

Chapter Seventeen

Leeds, Yorkshire, UK
5th of December, 6:55 a.m. (GMT)

Shyam Bhatt left his house at 6:55 on the dot, driving to the university for his 8:30 a.m. class on the Mughal Empire. Wilson followed two cars behind him under the guise of another commuter on his way to work. The Mine had given him the location of the faculty parking for the School of History as well as the make, model, and license of Bhatt's auto, but he wanted a chance to observe him before making contact.

Bhatt was a British national that was ethnically Indian and specialized in the history of the subcontinent before the Raj period. In his late fifties, he was on the short and slim side with just the hint of a belly but a full head of lush, wavy black hair. He dressed and drove conservatively and hospitably waved to his neighbor on the way out of the driveway.

Wilson waited for visual confirmation that Bhatt had entered the Michael Sadler Building, home of the School of History, before searching for his metallic white Maserati Ghibli in the parking garage. He'd done enough of these to know people had a penchant to bolt. In the proverbial sense, they always tried to close the barn door after the horses had gotten out. If Bhatt had an accomplice, they would be the first person he called. If he had a hideout, he would made a beeline straight for it. It was unlikely that Bhatt would think to ditch his car at the university, and if he did, that would also let Wilson know what kind of man he was dealing with.

With a small twist, Wilson turned on one of his bugs and quickly wedged it in between the car and the back license plate before hustling away. He checked his phone to make sure the software was working before crossing the campus to attend Dr. Bhatt's lecture. He'd get a better bead on the man after he observed him in his element.

Wilson's damp shoes squeaked on the industrial laminate flooring of the Michael Sadler Building. Architecturally speaking, it wasn't the oldest or prettiest of buildings on campus, but it had plenty of offices and classroom space, including large lecture rooms with full media. The halls were sparsely populated this early in the morning, and most of the students present were streaming into Bhatt's class.

Wilson waited in the corridor, catching glimpses of the lecture hall each time the double doors opened for undergrads whose backpacks were so weighed down they resembled turtles. It was a large enough space for Wilson to slip in unnoticed, especially since attendance was high this close to the end of the semester—everyone wanted hints as to what would be covered on the exams.

Wilson sat behind a tall young man and waited for the

class to start. Dr. Bhatt stood in the front at a lectern with an outline projected on the white screen on the wall. When the clock's hand clicked 8:30 a.m., Dr. Bhatt started talking and the class quieted immediately, lest they miss something important. Wilson had to hand it to Bhatt—he was punctual and had his ducks in a row. There was a constant tapping from those that took notes on laptops and tablets, and the young man in front of Wilson frantically typed every word that came out of Dr. Bhatt's mouth. Wilson could count the number of students taking written notes on his hands.

The organization and flow of Bhatt's lecture was smooth and seamless. This morning, Bhatt was discussing the various factors that contributed to the precipitous decline of the empire in the eighteenth century that ultimately laid the foundation for the British Raj after the failed Indian Rebellion of 1857. He stuck to the outline, and he had a habit of repeating important things twice, which the student in front of Wilson immediately bolded.

While Wilson enjoyed history, he wasn't there to hear Bhatt's perspective on the Mughal Empire. He was there to magically probe him while he was otherwise preoccupied. Teaching was a performative act with the students in attendance. Sometimes it was a monologue, other times it was improv, but it was always an interaction between speaker and audience. Bhatt was speaking from a place of passion, albeit thinly veiled in a veneer of scholastic distance, which made his lecture more like storytelling. His emotional connection to the subject was apparent to Wilson and made it all the easier for him to thread his will down the steps unnoticed. By the time Bhatt got to the deindustrialization of the later 1700s, Wilson had a good idea of what he was dealing with and stayed for the rest of the performance.

Bhatt ended the class at 9:20 a.m. and reiterated his office hours for anyone that had questions. The room erupted in conversation and noise as people packed up their things to haul to the next class. Wilson slipped out with the pack and headed to the second floor where Dr. Bhatt's office was located. As he suspected, there were no wards on the locked door.

People tended to compartmentalize their lives, and practitioners were no exception. They would ward where they practice magic and where they lived, but few thought to magically protect their cubicle or office against fiends, fae, ghosts, or other magicians. They were more likely to put something in place to keep the chatty coworker at bay or the smell of burnt popcorn or microwaved fish from entering their airspace.

Wilson took a seat and summoned his will, putting his esoteric protections in place. It was a precaution he took when he knew he was going up against another practitioner, regardless of their skill level. You could do all the recon and probing, but they were still people and capable of guile and surprising resourcefulness when cornered.

Bhatt came up the stairs with his briefcase and nodded to Wilson, who sat on the opposite side of the hall. Wilson waited until he fished out his keys, opened the door, and entered his office before addressing him. "Dr. Bhatt?"

"Yes, I am Dr. Bhatt." The man turned to address him after putting his things down on his desk. "How can I help you?"

Wilson stood and walked toward his office. "I attended your lecture this morning. I was wondering if I could have a moment of your time?"

He quickly surveyed the room. Bhatt's office was small, composed of a single stout wooden desk and two chairs for guests. The side walls were lined with bookcases groaning under the weight of their dust-jacketed titles. On the wall behind his desk were a few diplomas, a calendar displaying an image of the Mughal-built Red Fort in New Delhi, and several framed photos of Bhatt crossing finish lines.

"I'm afraid I have some work to do, but I have office hours this afternoon from 1:00-3:00," he answered firmly. "You're more than welcome to return then."

"You're a runner?" he asked the professor, pointing to the pictures. The inquiry had its intended effect of putting Bhatt at ease long enough to get in the room.

The professor gave him a genuine smile. "I run marathons in my spare time."

"I too have recently taken up running. It's very meditative," Wilson made conversation as he stepped inside.

"That's nice," Bhatt said dismissively as he took a seat at his desk. "As I said before, office hours are 1:00-3:00. Please close the door behind you."

Wilson did close the door behind him, only he was still inside the room. "I'm not one of your students, Dr. Bhatt. I'm here to ask about your extracurricular activities."

Even though Bhatt was two inches taller and forty pounds heavier than Wilson, he felt diminished under his gaze. "Who are you and what do you want?" His perfect Received Pronunciation took on a tone of righteous indignation that only the British could muster in the face of rudeness.

Wilson kept his position at the door. "I'm here to collect for Paul Youngblood, Zadie Gourlay, Asher Leek, and Jennifer Drake."

Bhatt's eyes darted to the closed door, and once he realized that Wilson was deliberately standing between him and it, returned to his visitor. Wilson felt the professor's will wash over him, as if a cold fog had suddenly blown by. "I believe you've confused me with someone else. I've never heard those names before."

Wilson pushed back with his will. "And I believe you've confused me with someone of lesser skill, Dr. Bhatt. I'll repeat the names for you. Paul Youngblood. Zadie Gourlay. Asher Leek. Jennifer Drake," his voice tightened on each syllable until the last one popped like a plucked string on an instrument.

"Four lives you cut short with these." He threw one of the empty blister packs he'd destroyed last night onto the desk. "Did you think you could do what you did without attracting the attention of the sharks that patrol the waters? Did you think that no one *pays attention*?"

He saw the panic in the professor's round brown eyes. "Don't worry, Dr. Bhatt. If I wanted to kill you, you wouldn't have made it to your 8:30 class. Shall we sit down and discuss this like gentlemen?"

Bhatt mutely nodded, and Wilson took one of the chairs between Bhatt and the exit. "As I was saying, there is a debt to be paid, but I'm not an unreasonable man. How you choose to settle accounts is up to you." Wilson opened his jacket and displayed the butt of his Glock 26. "But it *will* be paid."

Dr. Bhatt raised his hands up and protested, "It was never my intent for those students to die."

"And just what was your intent?" Wilson asked pointedly as he let his jacket hang to the side. Bhatt breathed a little easier with the gun out of sight and the opportunity to explain himself.

"It was supposed to re-route just a bit of intelligence—a little mental computing time, if you will—from English people to those they have wronged. Are you aware of the real history of Britain, Mr.…?"

"My name isn't important," Wilson said flatly.

"As you wish," Bhatt nervously replied. "Are you aware of what the British have *done*?"

"What have they done, Dr. Bhatt?" Although Wilson had a good understanding of world history, he played ignorant for the benefit of getting more out of the professor, whose emotional state made it more likely for him to be forthcoming.

Bhatt saw a chance at redemption, if only he could just make his uninvited visitor understand. "They murdered millions of my fellow Indians while they raped us of our wealth for their greedy nation's benefit. Under British rule, Indian exports fell from twenty-seven percent of the world's exports—twenty seven!—to a miniscule two percent. In modern terms, that's like the economies of China, the USA, and Germany being brought down to the export power of only Switzerland.

"In that time, their vaunted Empire—of which nearly fifty percent of Britons *still* fondly look back upon—deliberately killed at least twice as many Indians than the Jews killed by Nazis. From the eighteenth to the twentieth century, there were over a dozen famines in British-controlled India, all while the East India Company destroyed food crops and ordered cash crops to be planted: indigo, jute, and opium—which they used to enslave the Chinese, by the way!

"What food was allowed to be grown in the Indian subcontinent was exported to England at a low price and to other countries for a profit. They even exported food during the famines: the 1866 famine that killed four or five million, a third of the population of Orissa; the famine of 1876 that resulted in another five to ten million deaths; the 1896 famine that claimed a million lives; and the 1899 famine, where yet another million were—"

"I get the picture—they were monstrous," Wilson cut his oration short.

"*No!*" Bhatt nearly shouted. "If you are here to murder me because I had the temerity to accidently kill four"—he held up as many fingers to emphasize his point—"just four British people while seeking some sort of justice for hundreds of years of deliberate and malicious evil perpetrated against millions of innocent people, you will at least listen to what I have to say before doing it."

"No, I won't," Wilson said as he released his will, busting through Bhatt's limited magical defenses and freezing his vocal cords. "I'm well aware of the horrors that the British Empire inflicted upon the Indians, the Irish, the Boers, the Chinese, and countless other peoples as well as its role in the permanent scar on humanity that was the Atlantic slave trade, Dr. Bhatt. I am neither ignorant nor indifferent to the past and its impact on the present. But that's not why I'm here.

"I'm here because you failed the instant you drew our attention, Dr. Bhatt. Had you more skill and eluded our detection while using magic in your attempt at justice, I wouldn't be here. And now, you have one choice: work for us or die." Wilson tightened his will around Bhatt's throat for a few seconds to drive his point home and then released it.

The professor reflexively inhaled deeply and coughed. Then, he rubbed his throat and looked nervously side-to-side. "Who is us?"

"We are the Salt Mine."

Chapter Eighteen

North York Moors National Park, Yorkshire, UK
5th of December, 6:50 p.m. (GMT)

Bhatt managed to finish his day at the university, holding office hours and teaching his afternoon class, before driving off in his Maserati, but instead of heading home, he had taken a long and winding route through Yorkshire's wilderness. Wilson had kept his distance and used his phone to track his movements, suspecting Bhatt would be more vigilant about his rearview mirror after their conversation.

That was how Wilson found himself back in the moors, buried deep in the cold and dewy heather observing a hunting cabin through his binoculars. Although it was only five miles from where he'd hunted the previous morning, it was a far cry from the opulence of the Leek's Hunting House. Primitively built in the rustic style, the cabin was a long low structure no more than fifteen feet wide, but double that in length. It had originally belonged to Bhatt's paternal grandfather, but the professor inherited it eleven years ago after his father's death.

A single light gleamed from one of the back rooms, and it

drew Wilson's attention like a beacon. He ran his binoculars over the structure, memorizing entrances, exits, and any paths in the deeper moors that he could pick out of the background before he approached. He carefully walked toward the cabin, taking cover where he could. Closing the distance took longer than he cared, but there was no way to park closer without tipping off Bhatt to his presence. He kept his footing on the rough, uneven ground and was halfway there when the light in the front room lit up.

Wilson crouched down and brought his binoculars up to peer through the partially opened blinds. Bhatt, now casually dressed, was moving furniture. He pushed couches, chairs, and lamps to the side, clearing the center of the room. Then, he dragged a large round table from the back room. Given how many breaks Bhatt took and the exasperated look on his face as he rested his hands on his thighs, it was heavy. Once the table was in the center of the room, Bhatt reached underneath and released a latch. The tabletop flipped on an axis, revealing an inlaid summoning circle on the other side.

Shit, Wilson cursed. He recognized the circle instantly; Bhatt was communicating with demons. Fiends were bad news, and demons the worst of them. They were duplicitous evil beings that said whatever was necessary to get what they wanted. As chaotic creatures, they were not bound to the promises they made, which meant summoners had to be strong enough to bind them and smart enough to resist their honeyed words. Only the most skilled magicians could come out ahead in a bargain with a demon.

Wilson ran over the possibilities. Bhatt could be summoning a knowledgeable demon to get more information about the Salt Mine. The cost was high—nothing short of the summoner's blood—but Wilson had more than one such demon in his arcane rolodex when the need arose. Perhaps Bhatt had consulted a demon about the scheme with the caffeine pills and this was effectively him calling his accomplice at the first possible moment? Or maybe Bhatt was simply summoning a demon to kill Wilson. It was that thought that propelled him to the cabin.

Bhatt still had to set up the accoutrements before he could start the summoning, and Wilson hustled as best he could on the uneven ground, using a circuitous route that kept him out of sight of the windows. The front of the cabin went dark as Bhatt switched off the lights and lit a multitude of candles he'd placed on the ground around the table. It was all the time Wilson needed to close the gap. Taking partial cover behind the Maserati, he took position under the passenger window and listened. He could hear Bhatt's voice but couldn't make out distinct words.

Taking a calculated risk, he bear-crawled around the car and then under the main front window of the cabin. This time, Bhatt's incantation clearly came through the old, single-paned glass. "The darkness is here, terrible and quiet. The quiet is here, dark and terrible. The terror is here, quiet and dark. The hunger is here, cold and endless. Eternity is here, hungry and cold. The cold is here, eternal and hungry…" Wilson recognized the beginning of a tripartite summoning; he had time.

Tripartite summonings worked by merging three concepts into one and then blurring the lines between the individual and the collective until the three were one and the one was three—like how a trident is one, yet three, yet still one. They used to be employed in early Christian magic, but they fell out of favor a few centuries after Christianity reached Europe. However, they were still common in South Asian and Southeast Asian practices.

Tripartite summonings were long and rigidly constructed, and the being to be summoned was always named in the last verse in tripartite structure—first in opposition and then joined to the concepts of "earth" and "air." Now, all he had to do was get his Glock ready—which was loaded with banishment bullets—and see if Bhatt called the demon by its common name or a true name.

Every fiend, devil and demon alike, had a true name, something that captured the very essence of the creature, the pure distillation of the entirety of their existence. True names were double-edged swords to the infernals. The more locations where their true name was known, the greater power it received; true-name dispersion was the root of more than one devil's ascension up the ranks, although it almost inevitably resulted in a subsequent fall.

Knowing a true name gave a practitioner nearly complete power over fiends, provided the magician knew what to do with such information and had time to properly prepare—think Rumpelstiltskin with more sulfur and aether. Fiends could be wracked with pain, blinded, rendered mute, and even imprisoned permanently in a magical prison. Wilson was pretty sure that's how Leader trapped Furfur—not that that was his true name—but he'd never had the nerve to ask for confirmation.

Knowing a demon's true name was just about the only way a practitioner could bend it to their will, and he would have newfound respect for Bhatt's skills if the professor had one. Whenever a practitioner read or learned the name of a fiend in study, it was more than likely a common name which conferred some power because the naming of things was always an exercise in power, but more akin to a nickname than a true name. True names were closely guarded secrets, and Wilson knew only two after years of study and prolonged exposure to the infernal world.

As Bhatt continued his strident chanting, Wilson had hard decisions to make. If he wanted to safely interrupt Bhatt, he needed to do it before he was halfway into the ritual; after that, disrupting the summoning could have unforeseen circumstances. Wilson weighed the pros and cons and finally settled upon letting things play out: the chance to learn a true name didn't come around every day, and Leader really wanted her informant.

By the time Bhatt reached the ninth section of the tripartite incantation—the third three—Wilson's heart was pounding in his chest. He pressed his shoulder against the rough wooden side of the cabin, tilting and turning his ear toward the single pane to try and catch every last nuance of pronunciation.

"The quiet is here, airless and earthless. The airless is here, earthless and quiet. The airless is here, quiet and earthless. I call you from Antarik☒a! I call you from beyond earth, from beyond air! I call you, Pretakhuni!"

Wilson's veins lit up with magical charge as Bhatt enunciated the final syllable: it was the energy that belonged to only one thing. *It is a true name!* he silently crowed, even as he wracked his brain for any knowledge about Pretakhuni. As he tried to recall the name, the first wave of the summoning hit him even though he was outside the cabin. The presence of a manifested demon made itself known to those with magical ability.

Demons were so out of place in the mortal realm that they warped the fabric of reality, like putting a bowling ball on a trampoline, and Wilson was close to the epicenter. He felt pulled, no stretched, toward the summoning circle. Demons could control the warp they caused but only at great effort and pain on their part. They would much rather take possession of a human or animal, and even that was only a temporary shield. Mortal flesh was not meant to contain them any more than the mortal realm was.

"I am here, master," Pretakhuni announced in a glassy baritone.

Bhatt spit out his reply, "I am wroth with you, demon. You lied to me."

Wilson rolled his eyes and stifled a groan. Apparently Bhatt was one of *those* magicians. Over the years, he'd encountered dozens of tiresome practitioners who felt the need for embellished language when working magic, as if using *thees* and *thous* would somehow elevate their magic to new heights of solemnity. Wilson understood the impulse, but there wasn't anything special or holy about magic; magic just *was* and you did it right or you suffered the consequences.

"What have I done to offend, great master?" the demon wheedled.

"You said no one would be greatly harmed by our magic."

Our magic? Wilson noted. It was Bhatt's signature that showed up on the pills, not the demon's. Bhatt should be in control of the demon with its true name, meaning that a shared magic should have revealed at least some influence of Pretakhuni in the signature. Wilson started to wonder if Pretakhuni was pulling the strings.

"That is true. Our magic is incapable of causing such harm," the demon swore vehemently.

"So how then have four people died?" Bhatt pressed.

"If they did not die of natural causes, they must have

injured themselves or had someone else injure them, great one," the fiend spun a web of words. Wilson scoffed; it was defense without denying wrongdoing.

"The Salt Mine doesn't think so," Bhatt stated as fact, but even Wilson could hear the doubt creep into his voice.

"O great master, the Salt Mine is not to be trusted! It is an organization of selfish and evil beings. Everything they say is twisted to their own purposes," Pretakhuni cajoled he who summoned him. "Have there even been deaths, great master? Are they not above lying about everything?"

That's rich, coming from a demon! Wilson stewed to himself.

"I didn't check them all," Bhatt admitted, "but I recognized one name and he did die."

"Mortals die every day, master," the demon reasoned. "You should check them all. But even if there were four deaths, isn't that a small price for justice?" Wilson didn't like Bhatt's silence. "The Salt Mine scares you so they can use you and steal your power. You know how they are."

"I know all too well," Bhatt stated emphatically.

Wilson shook his head as Bhatt's last statement solidified the subtextural nature of the conversation. *What kind of idiot manages to get charmed when he has a demon's true name!* He quietly sighed; he was going to have to go in. A magician charmed by a demon wasn't going to stop doing what the demon wanted. Bhatt might not even be the real mastermind behind the pills to begin with.

There were many ways to break a charm, and Wilson was confident that he would win in an extended battle of wills with Bhatt, but he didn't want to chance it while a demon lurked only a few feet away, as there was the chance of releasing the demon by taking away Bhatt's focus. That meant he had to send the demon home first.

Wilson's reached for his Glock and then remembered he was loaded for European and North African duty. His subcontinental banishing bullets were in his rental parked nearly a mile away.

He wracked his brain and had another idea in seconds. *Okay, let's try Plan C.* He cleared his mind and gathered his will—*think, think, think*. He spooled out a line of it and knitted it into a mesh, something he could toss over Bhatt, and then looped the end through the structure, like a fishing net. If his theory was right, it should act like an esoteric Faraday cage over the professor. It would instantly sever the magical current flowing from the charmer to charmed without automatically triggering any natural defenses of the charmed.

Once his net was ready, he took a deep breath, dashed up the small front porch, and pushed hard against the thin door of the cabin. Bhatt was on his knees on a towel on the far end of the room, ceremonial dagger in his right hand. His left shirtsleeve was rolled up, and a thin trail of blood ran down it from where he'd pricked himself with the dagger. Between them was the summoning circle containing Pretakhuni.

The demon was as dark as obsidian and tall, towering over Wilson by several feet. Its long limbs—two legs and six clawed arms—were emaciated, as was the rest of the body, including a distended potbelly. Throughout its body, veins bulged, twisted, and intertwined like a river fresh off a glacier. It turned away from Bhatt when Wilson burst through the door; its two pairs of eyes bore into him. The bottom pair was twice as large as human eyes and blood red, but the top pair was human-sized, with piercing blue pupils and crimson where the whites should have been.

Wilson launched his charm-breaker and cried out, "It's charmed you!" before either could react further. The woven mesh of Wilson's will whirled above Pretakhuni's lumpy head and landed perfectly on Bhatt. Wilson pulled on the cord and it closed as designed. Bhatt's face changed the instant the sphere sealed around him, and he looked disjointed, as if he'd suddenly come to from a long daydream.

Pretakhuni howled and tried to reclaim its puppet. "You cannot trust him, great master! You cannot trust him!" Each arm clashed against the field of power formed by the summoning circle, sending cerulean sparks into the air.

Bhatt stood and stared at Wilson, muddied and wet from his travel across the moor, and then at Pretakhuni, raving and slavering long strings of bloody mucus. "Silence!" Bhatt commanded the demon before addressing Wilson, "You followed me?"

"It didn't feel like you were telling me the whole truth back in your office, so I had to be sure everything was as it seemed," Wilson said diplomatically. "I *did* break the demon's charm over you." He readied his will as he tested the waters, uncertain if it was the charm that had set them in opposition or if there were deeper seas of conflict between them.

Bhatt's rose from his knees, and Wilson cautiously eyed the dagger still in his hand. "I see. It seems I personally owe you, then." He looked down and sighed. "I always pay my debts."

Silence ruled for a second and then the professor looked Wilson directly in the eyes. He'd seen such a look only once before, from a man who'd just decided to jump off a bridge. Bhatt tossed the dagger up and took to his heels, racing for the back door of the cabin.

From Wilson's perspective, the blade arced in slow motion, tip over end. It descended toward the summoning circle that separated the men from the demon. And then, with an audible pop and ripple, it landed and the circle was broken.

Chapter Nineteen

North York Moors National Park, Yorkshire, UK
5th of December, 7:35 p.m. (GMT)

Wilson's finger double-tapped the trigger of his Glock while the demon was more focused on Bhatt's retreat—best case, Pretakhuni was multicultural and would return to hell; worst case, he took regular firearm damage. The familiar kick punched through the silence and both shots found their target. The first landed just below the neck and the second hit the center of mass. Each bullet gouged small ebony chunks out of the creature, and much to Wilson's dismay, the demon did not disappear. Worse, it didn't even flinch. The points of impact hissed and dissipated air before reforming. *Shit! Of course it's an amorphous fiend.*

Amorphous fiends were a type of infernal that appeared solid, but were more akin to a non-Newtonian fluid. They were formed of stuff that behaved sort of like oobleck—that ever-popular science experiment with cornstarch and water—but their components were evil and had an unquenchable desire for souls. Most amorphous fiends were demons, but not exclusively, and the really nasty ones were also shapeshifters.

Their unique form effectively made them immune to high-kinetic attacks, like bullets. Without the proper banishment sigils, his bullets would do little more than draw the attention of its four blood-red eyes, which moved independently, like a chameleon's. Slow-velocity weaponry, such as hand-to-hand weapons, would be more effective, but fighting melee with a demon wasn't on Wilson's bucket list, and he'd already technically died twice.

At a loss of what to do next, Wilson fired another two shots before diving out the front door and legging it. One hit the demon in the face and the other hit its suprasternal notch. They were little more than a pesky annoyance and it laughed gleefully. Long had Pretakhuni suffered Bhatt's insufferable prattle, and it savored its newfound freedom in the mortal realm.

With the circle broken, the existential pain of the mortal realm rejecting his very presence pressed against it. It would only have a few minutes on this plane before it would have to return to hell unless he took possession of a human. The demon quickly made up his mind: take possession of one, and then devour as much as he could before having to change man-suits.

Instinctually, Bhatt was the obvious choice. It'd already established a connection with him once, and there was no love lost for the magician who had bound and summoned it with its true name. But the other one was at least trying to fight, and it did like a feisty meal. It sniffed the air to help in its decision, and noticed that the interloper smelled extremely tempting. There was great power there, and something spiced his soul unlike anything the demon had smelled before. It had been so long since it had played with something novel. After a moment's decision, Pretakhuni made for the porch in pursuit of Wilson, knuckling it like a gorilla.

Outside, Wilson holstered his gun and desperately yanked Andvaranaut from its necklace, sending silver links of chain flying across the damp wood of the porch. The uncomfortably heavy ring found his finger, and he hastily wove a thread of will around his right hand and wrist as a boxer would before a fight. He flattened himself against the wall of the cabin, fear rising, and chose his moment carefully. *Think, think, think.*

The instant the demon's head broke the doorway, Wilson drove his full weight against it. He was a good boxer and knew how and where to land a punch, but neither he nor the demon expected the damage to follow. Pretakhuni went down hard face-first into the pine boards; it felt like someone had dropped an anvil on its face, and its screams filled the moors. Not waiting, Wilson immediately sprinted down the driveway. He knew the demon wouldn't be so easy to punch a second time, now that they were both aware of what Wilson was capable of with Andvaranaut on his hand. Instead, he would follow Bhatt's example of running away.

Pretakhuni grunted, groggily shook its head, and rose to its feet. The smell of the human's big magic was smeared over him, and he wanted it more than before. It launched itself after the small man, charging like a silverback, faster than a human could run.

Wilson looked over his shoulder and saw the demon gaining on him. He wasn't going to be able to outrun it, so he turned to face it. He squeezed his fist over Andvaranaut—*All I want is for it to jump at me, arms open. Arms open!* Wilson felt the ring feed on his will.

"Pretakhuni, I name you and order you flee," he called out as the demon rapidly closed. It wasn't a powerful naming, but it was still a naming, and Wilson grasped at all the straws he had.

The demon felt its strength drain a measure, reducing the time it had in the mortal realm, but it still had enough to get what it wanted. It laughed. "I will enjoy wearing you, human." It closed the final few yards with a leap, arms wide open.

At the last possible second, Wilson dropped to the ground like a rock, letting gravity pull him down without contest. As he fell, he kicked up his legs, threading the six clawed arms that hadn't yet reacted to his change of position. His feet found purchase on the distended stomach of the demon and he used it as a springboard, lifting the demon upward and onward, over Wilson's head.

Pretakhuni was stunned by the maneuver; however had the puny mortal accomplished such a thing? As the fiend spun forward, Wilson used its momentum to perform a backroll before he scrambled to his feet and raced away in a dead sprint in the opposite direction. This time, his sights were on Bhatt's Maserati right outside the cabin. The earth under his feet trembled as the creature hit the ground.

Wilson yanked on the unlocked door handle and climbed into the driver's seat. He knew how to hotwire a car, but with no tools and no time, he turned to Andvaranaut instead. *All I want is for this car to start. All I want is for this car to start,* Wilson pleaded as he pressed the ignition button. His adrenaline was at full throttle as the black shadow of the demon was nearing, and he could hear it scrabbling on the gravel for more traction before launching itself toward the car.

The Ghibli's engine purred to life, and the headlights automatically turned on. He crammed the stick into reverse, peeling out and under the leaping demon, whose muddy claws found no traction on the metallic white hood of the car. The high beams cast the demon in stark light as the distance between them increased. Wilson pushed the engine as far as it would go and steered using the rearview mirror; he dared not turn his head away from the fiend. Just as he was making plans on where to drive, two explosive pops reverberated through the vehicle and the car jerked as both back tires lost air and flattened.

Goddamn it! Wilson cursed. Of all the times for karma to call in its markers, it had to be now. He had no idea how much he'd burned, but it had to be a significant deficit for it to hit so quickly. Of course, the amount was a moot point if he died now, be it from demon or karmic backlash. "Why not both?" he said with gallows humor as he shifted out of reverse and jammed the car into first. The engine squealed at the abuse.

With Pretakhuni closing in fast, the fear he'd experienced in the blackness of the Japanese mine returned. He pushed it down and did the only thing he could do—he pressed on the accelerator and slammed into the onrushing demon. The front end crumpled, pinning Pretakhuni underneath. The demon cried out from the impact, Wilson hoped in pain but he'd settle for frustration. Apparently, a head-on collision with a car whose back tires were blown counted as a low-velocity impact.

Wilson ground the car out of gear and dove out, darting for the cabin. As he passed the front of the Maserati, one of the demon's arms reached out. A claw slid against his right leg, cleanly slicing through the fabric but missing flesh by a hair's breadth. He was on the porch when the sound of tearing metal screeched behind him—the demon finally freeing itself from the Maserati. It was worse than fingernails across a chalkboard and sent a shiver down his spine, but he kept his eyes on the cabin.

At least I ruined the bastard's car, he thought spitefully as his wet shoes slipped on the waxed flooring of the summoning room. He grabbed Bhatt's ceremonial dagger, flipped over the table, and readied for the coming demon. The candlelight around the table gave the room a soft glow, and his heart raced at the crunch of gravel.

As the seconds ticked by, something snapped and his magic exploded without warning or deliberate intent. Endless spools of will wrapped around his body like vines, and he thought it a form of magical attack until he realized the energy was coming from within. A shifting layer of arcane protection instantaneously grew to cover him from crown to sole, and he felt nigh invincible.

The demon crossed the threshold, each of its four eyes scanning a different part of the room for its quarry. They all synced as it locked onto Wilson's location, and the fiend's powerful legs launched it toward him once more. This time, it held out its six arms to cover all directions: there would be no escaping its grasp.

Within his magical armor, time slowed and Wilson found himself moving faster than human. Pretakhuni seemed to hang in the air in front of him. He didn't know what was happening, but he took full advantage of it, diving at the demon while concentrating his will. "Pretakhuni, I name you. Die!"

He stabbed the dagger into and out of one of its large eyes and an infernal wail erupted. *That one hurt*, Wilson noted with smug satisfaction. Then he slid underneath its body, raking the underside with the blade. Thick, black ichor beaded along the laceration. Once he cleared the creature, Wilson took to his feet and raised the dagger, ready for retaliation.

But there was none. Pretakhuni fell slowly and before it hit the pine floor, its body had already hissed and dissipated into a sulfurous black haze. As the demon faded to nothingness, Wilson held up his hands to examine the golden magical armor that had encased him, but it too was evaporating into a twinkly shower of golden sparks. He stared in silence for a while. "That's another one for the list," he said to the empty cabin.

He righted the table and rested the dagger on in while he pulled out his phone and texted a message to the Mine: *Karma hit, need immediate support.* The text automatically caused a $5,000 donation to be sent to one of the many charities the Mine supported. Had he been using someone else's phone, he would have had to add a nine-digit code for identification, but since it came from his number, there was no need.

He pocketed the phone and picked up the dagger. *Now, for unfinished business.*

Chapter Twenty

North York Moors National Park, Yorkshire, UK
5th of December, 7:35 p.m. (GMT)

Shyam Bhatt sprinted out of the cabin and onto a trail leading deeper into the moors. The door slammed behind him but he didn't stop to look back. His mind was still a little fuzzy, but he knew he didn't want to be stuck between a freed demon and the guy who'd earlier threatened to kill him—of this he was sure. He was a fanatical runner familiar with the terrain; he'd run these paths in good weather and bad for years. By his reckoning, he'd circle back around after a brief mile and see where things were. It shouldn't take long for Pretakhuni to take care of his unwanted guest, and then he could return and exert his power using its true name.

He'd just cleared the ridge leading to the moors proper when the second round of gunfire popped off. *Who brings a gun to fight an infernal?* Bhatt chided Wilson from afar. The professor was rather pleased with his quick thinking, and now that he knew the Salt Mine was onto him, he could take precautions. As he ran along the ridge, he heard a bellow ripple across the landscape. He froze in place. *That wasn't human.*

He took cover and knelt behind the wet heather brush. It hadn't rained in hours, but the ground was rarely dry this time of year. This was the nature of the moors. His eyes adjusted to the dim moonlight and he turned his attention to the cabin. Bhatt watched the shadows in combat and retreat. The pure blackness of Pretakhuni followed the man sprinting down the driveway. *With even just a little distance, everything looks like ants*, he lorded from his lofty perch.

Bhatt's smirk soon vanished when the man threw the demon overhead and ran back toward the cabin. His brain refused to believe his eyes. Pretakhuni should have torn him to shreds, but the man was faster. Such a thing was inconceivable. *He must be a powerful practitioner*, Bhatt postured a supposition. *But no matter, it is only a matter of time until the demon devours his soul, whatever he is*, the professor comforted himself.

His mood darkened as soon as he saw what became of his beloved Maserati—crushed like a soda can, with the demon pinned underneath. As Pretakhuni freed itself, Bhatt could hear the sheering of metal all the way up there. A knot formed in his gut and his confidence was starting to waver. *Surely, Pretakhuni will finish the job...*

It was difficult to make out what was going on inside the cabin; all Bhatt saw were shadows upon shadows, but he knew all was lost when a blood-curdling shriek sounded in the night.

Bhatt not only heard it; he felt it in his soul. And then he saw Wilson exit the structure.

There was only one thought in his mind: *Run!* Bhatt quietly backed away from the ridge and took off on the wet trail. When he felt certain he couldn't be seen from the cabin, he hazarded a little light and checked his phone. His thumbs slid on the screen, looking for the bus schedule and the nearest stop. He had to get out of the country—somewhere he could lie low and regroup—but that required a stop at his home in Leeds. He'd need his passport at the very least, and he was of the generation that still kept a stash of hard currency for emergencies. In his experience, everyone took cash.

The buses ran less frequently out in the country, especially at night. He noted the time and his current location before picking his destination. If he missed the 8:15, there would be another before the end of the night, and there was always a chance of catching a taxi. With something to run toward, he put his phone away and reflexively looked behind him. In the moonlight, he saw a silhouette crest the ridge. *It couldn't be him?* Bhatt objected intellectually, but in his heart, he knew it was. The figure was heading straight for him.

Bhatt knew it was too late to turn himself in and agree to cooperate. If the Salt Mine took issue with four dead university students, they wouldn't look kindly on summoning a demon and setting it loose on their representative. Terrified, the professor took off at full speed, fleeing from the armed man who had just defeated a demon and had somehow located him on a remote trail in the dark Yorkshire moors.

*****

The path through the moors was slippery in places, and Wilson found himself having to concentrate more upon his footing than on the distant shadow of Bhatt. He'd considered going back for his rental, but he didn't want to risk losing the professor. While the battle with Pretakhuni seemed like an eternity, it was over in minutes and he figured Bhatt couldn't have had much of a head start. Using the summoner's blood on the dagger, Wilson was able to get a fix on his general direction, and with high ground and a break in the cloud cover, he'd spotted him.

He'd hoped his initial burst of speed would be enough to overtake the magician, or at very least bring him into reliable range of his Glock, but it had proved insufficient. Once Bhatt knew he was being pursued, he picked up his pace. The professor was roughly a hundred and fifty yards ahead, and they had settled into a long-distance chase. *Good idea, Agent Fulcrum*, he sarcastically scolded himself between breaths. *Let's get in a footrace with a marathoner in the dark through the moors. That will look great on the report.*

He briefly considered using Andvaranaut to close the gap, but quickly shut such thoughts down. *This is why I don't like magic rings*, he grumbled as he navigated his way through the brush. They beckoned to be used, and the good ones made it seem like it was your idea. He still had the ring on his finger. With the chain busted, there was no way to secure it with easy access should he really need it. He'd considered sliding it into a pocket, but he could only image the wrath Chloe and Dot would bring down on him if he lost it. Much less Leader.

Despite his initial aversion, he was glad Chloe had forced him to take it. He ran over how much of a role Andvaranaut had played in the last fight. By all rights, Pretakhuni should have killed him, or worse, possessed him and used his skills to wreck more havoc. Wilson had always said he would rather end it than be possessed; he'd worked too hard to regain his soul for it to be fiend chow. But he knew all too well that practitioners didn't always have time to act accordingly—he'd had to put down more than one in his time.

There was one thing he couldn't blame on the ring: his spontaneous magical armor. He didn't know how he did it, only that it was something he had never done before and by all rights, shouldn't have been able to do. It was some next-level augmentation magic.

All Salt Mine agents were tutored in basic physical stabilization, the arcane equivalent of donning magical brass knuckles or sportsball pads. It helped them protect themselves from their own natural physical power, but it didn't add to the sum total of their abilities. But that was as far as most practitioners got; the higher-level augmentation spells required an innate aptitude that simply couldn't be taught. Except that somehow Wilson had just managed to supernaturally augment himself. For the briefest of moments, the sum was greater than the total.

The chill of the night started to take hold now that he had a sheen of sweat for the breeze to catch. Bhatt couldn't run forever, and he just had to stay on him. There was no doubt in his mind that he was going to have to kill the professor; a summoner tainted by demonic forces wasn't an asset Leader could use. Slowly, he gained a little ground when the terrain was in his favor, speeding up downhill and keeping pace uphill. Bhatt was only a hundred yards out now, but if he didn't catch him before he reached a populated area, things could get messy.

If Bhatt got somewhere where he could ask for help, Wilson would be hard pressed to explain his pistol, even with his Interpol cover. Worse would be if he was detained before he executed Bhatt; he would eventually be cleared and released, but not before the professor had a chance to slip away. Of course, he could always take out Bhatt and charm his way out of it, but that could become a large expenditure of magic depending on the number of witnesses…and he had already been on a karmic knife's edge once tonight.

A light flashed on Bhatt, and Wilson could see he was checking his phone. Wilson sensed an opportunity and started sprinting, closing the distance between them to eighty yards;

he was nothing if not relentless.

Chapter Twenty-One

Fylingthorpe, Yorkshire, UK
5th of December, 8:09 a.m. (GMT)

Bhatt checked the time on his phone—he had five and a half minutes to catch the 8:15 p.m. express service bus. Up to now, he'd relied on his conditioning, footwear, and familiarity with the surface of the paths, hoping that would be enough to shake off his pursuer, but each time he stole a glance over his shoulder, Wilson was there, edging ever closer.

Bhatt kept up the punishing pace. After cresting a hill, he took off at full speed to make the most of the brief moment he would be out of the agent's sight. Normally, he wouldn't take such risks, but he knew this was his last chance to make a clean break. Using a technique he'd discovered during his marathon competitions, he summoned his will and wrapped it around his feet and ankles as he made a mad dash down the long gentle slope, over the ridge, and onto the blessedly level paved road.

There was the occasional house, but all Bhatt could see was the glow of Fylingdale Inn. The parking lot was full and the double-decker bus was parked just opposite the restaurant's entrance. The driver was outside chatting with a dinner patron and finishing a cigarette. He started panicking when he saw the driver say his goodbyes and slowly amble back to his bus. *Please don't leave until the scheduled time!* he pleaded to the fates.

Drawing every bit of energy he had, Bhatt clipped the last corner, running through someone's lawn in the process, and hopped onto the bus just before the driver closed the door.

The driver stared at the puffing man, as did the thirteen mostly-elderly passengers. "Good evening," Bhatt greeted their stares with a polite smile as he dug into his pockets and paid the fare. He took a window seat away from the other passengers, and the driver rolled the bus northward. The digital sign up front changed as the bus sped off onto the dark road, and everyone settled in. The next stop was miles away.

"I guess he really couldn't wait for the next bus," he heard one of the old ladies behind him whisper to her friend.

*****

Wilson stopped to catch his breath as the two red dots of the bus receded from him. Apparently, Bhatt wasn't just a good endurance runner; he was also a sprinter. He pulled out his phone and let his thumbs do the work. By this point, Wilson had lost count on which letter of the alphabet he should name this plan. *Probably Plan H.*

He identified the bus as the express that ran from

Scarborough to Middlesbrough, making limited stops along the way. In sixteen minutes, it would stop in Whitby, where it would wait for five minutes before departing onward. Wilson sent another request for immediate karmic donation to the Mine; he needed to make the most out of the next sixteen minutes.

He scanned the cars in the parking lot and chose the most non-descript make and model—a white Vauxhall Corsa. He wanted to keep a low profile and make it harder for people to identify him via the car. A quick spell and he was inside and on the road in less than a minute. He turned on the lights and tested the limits of the car. Its performance was pathetic, but it was enough to catch up to the bus after six minutes of speeding and aggressively passing slower traffic.

When an opening came, he passed the chugging behemoth of a bus and breathed a sigh of relief when he saw Bhatt looking out the window into the darkness. Following the instructions on his phone, Wilson gained ground and raced ahead to the bus stop in Whitby, where he did a quick pass to assess security. He didn't see any cameras, but there was a half dozen people waiting for the bus, preoccupied with their phones or music.

He circled back around and parked. Using his phone, he looked up the nearest police station to estimate the response time as well as the closest public parking lot—a massive lot servicing the nearby marina. He used the ground view function and found a back entrance to the lot that appeared to lack cameras. With the bare bones of a plan in place, he exchanged his banishment bullet for nondescript 9mms. His hand rested on the Glock in his jacket and he waited.

The bus arrived as scheduled, passing Wilson's illegally parked car to bank into the stop. Once the back of the bus cleared the Corsa's front bumper, Wilson was out the door, casually walking along the sidewalk where passengers were exiting. Bhatt was the third to step out. He was still getting his bearings when two bullets ripped through his chest.

It took a second for people to register that someone had been shot, and that's when the screaming started. Everyone scattered and in the chaos, Wilson checked to make sure Bhatt was dead. Satisfied, he walked back to the Corsa and drove away. This time, he followed the speed limit and obeyed all the traffic laws; now was not the time to attract attention.

After a series of turns, he drove to the marina parking lot and entered through the back. He tooled around until he parked next to a suitable luxury vehicle; the white economy car looked even more pitiful next to the Jaguar. Before he abandoned it, Wilson cast an ancient cleaning spell on the exterior and interior of the car, removing all traces he may have left behind.

The drive back into the moors was smoother than his ride to Whitby. All he had to do now was get back to his rental, torch Bhatt's cabin which reeked of infernal aether, and quietly make his way to Heathrow with a stop in Leeds to gather his things from the hotel.

As the adrenaline wore off, Wilson became pensive. Now that he was no longer chasing Bhatt and fighting a demon, he could see how Bhatt would have made a good asset. He was intelligent, thought well on his feet, and Leader would have surely found a way to use his anger and sense of justice. It was too bad Pretakhuni had gotten to him.

It wasn't the resolution the Mine wanted, but it was the way the problem wanted to be solved.

Epilogue

York Hospital, Yorkshire, UK
7th of December, 7:15 p.m. (GMT)

"You call this dinner?" Cordelia Durand Leek asked indignantly as the tray lid was removed. "There's not even butter for the roll."

"Mrs. Leek, you've been put on a heart-healthy diet," the nurse replied firmly.

"I may have had a heart attack, but I assure you, my taste buds are still in working order," she replied brusquely.

Imogene looked up from her book. "It really doesn't look that bad, Cordelia."

"It's not how it looks—although it's not winning any awards for plating. It's how it tastes. Or rather, how it tastes like nothing," she huffed. "They won't even bring me a salt shaker."

"Heart-healthy diets are supposed to be low sodium and low fat," Imogene reasoned.

"Your sister-in-law is right," the nurse backed her up as she methodically reconciled each medication to Mrs. Leek's chart, double-checking the name and the dose. A kaleidoscope of shapes and colors landed in the paper cup for dispensing. "Plus, your medicine will go down better if you take it with food." The nurse handed Cordelia the cup with a glass of water. "Down the hatch."

"What's the point of surviving when you have to take a mountain of pills and you can't eat anything worth chewing?" the ornery patient asked rhetorically. She didn't approve of medication; she preferred a strong cup of tea and either a nap or a long constitutional walk for whatever ailed her.

Unaccustomed to swallowing pills, she took each tablet one at a time with a generous amount of water in between. She had to tilt her head back and shake it from side to side, giving it a straight shot down her throat. Cordelia made a face but they went down, by hook or by crook.

The nurse rewarded her with an approving nod. "Try to eat something," she recommended. "You'll need your strength to get home sooner."

The allusion to Buttercrambe Hall was enough to get her to begrudgingly pick up her fork and poke at the steamed chicken breast and limp green beans sans sauce or salt. Imogene gave the nurse a sly look, which she returned with a wink. "If you need anything, just press the call button," she stated before leaving the room.

Cordelia waited until the nurse left before taking a bite. She was hungry and if she got tired of chewing on the dry chicken, she could always eat the pudding. "What news from

Buttercrambe?" she made conversation as she sawed through her dinner.

"Everything's under control," Imogene said dutifully. "You just concentrate on getting better."

Cordelia was about to tell her closest confidant exactly what she thought about that answer when someone knocked on the door. The women exchanged glances. Imogene shrugged; tonight was her turn to sit with Cordelia.

"Come in," Cordelia called out. A large arrangement of flowers appeared at the door.

"More flowers, Mrs. Leek," the orderly informed her. Cordelia ran her eyes over the tasteful bouquet of gladiolus, a flower for remembrance, strength of character, and honor. She approved.

"Aren't they lovely," Imogene commented and grabbed the envelope once the vase was solidly placed on the windowsill. "Whoever could have sent them?"

An enigmatic smile crept onto her face as she read; it piqued Cordelia's curiosity. "Don't be mysterious. Go on, tell me who sent them," she chastised Imogene.

"Perhaps you should read it yourself," Imogene replied, handing her the card.

Cordelia held the small rectangle at arm's length before bringing it quite close to read the typed message: *Best wishes on your recovery. Rest easy knowing all are punished.* She flipped it over to see if there was a name or signature, but it was blank.

"Is there anything in the envelope?"

Imogene handed her the plain white slip. Cordelia turned it upside down and shook out its contents. A packet of salt fell out. Serenity came over Cordelia's face; Asher's murder had been avenged. Her softened eyes looked up at her sister-in-law. "Not a word to Daunty," she said quietly. "He wouldn't like it."

"No, of course not," Imogene replied.

Cordelia shook the packet and tore open one corner, carefully dispersing the white grains on her plate. "And not a word to the nurse," she said conspiratorially.

Imogene averted her gaze and innocently asked, "Tell them what?"

*****

"Look mommy, I'm inside the ball!" Claire yelled as she jumped up and down. Her face beamed as she looked up at the strings of bulbs, and giggles erupted as she spun in the sphere of lights. "Hurry up!" Allison hustled to catch up with her runaway daughter and posed on the path running through the giant Christmas ornament while Joan took a picture.

The Detroit Zoo did Wild Lights every year, but this was the first time Joan had ever been. It sounded more fun than driving through a bunch of Christmas lights, and Claire wasn't quite old enough to appreciate historic Greenfield Village. The little girl adored animals and never said no to a zoo trip, and she'd gone bananas when Joan suggested it to Allison. The fact that it was at night was even better; it made Claire feel very grown up.

"Now one with Aunt Jo," Claire requested. Joan swapped places with Allison and squatted down so she was roughly the same height as the four-and-a-half-year-old.

"Come on, kiddo," Joan put her hand on Claire's back. As she stood up, spots in her vision were sparkling from the flash. "Other people want to stand in the ornament, too." Allison joined them and together they stepped through the glittering display. She had one hand holding her daughter's and the other in Joan's.

"Look, it's a dragonfly!" Claire exclaimed and pointed with her free hand. "It's almost as big as me." She pulled them to one side, and patrons made way for the determined child filled with raw enthusiasm, giving her adult companions sympathetic smiles.

Although there were plenty of colorful lights all around, the night was quite dark, especially if one wandered off the trail. In the blackness between displays, Joan sensed a presence and instinctively summoned her will. It wasn't malevolent on first prod, but they were definitely being followed.

She turned to her troupe and made a suggestion. "You know, I think the insect and reptile houses are open for visitors. Why don't you and mommy go take a look and I'll rustle us some hot chocolate and meet you there?" Claire fully embraced the idea because it involved looking at real animals *and* hot chocolate. Allison didn't object because it got her out of the cold for a little bit.

Joan waved and smiled as they departed down the tunnel of lights. Once they were well on their way, her face turned serious as she addressed the dark. "Hi, Wilson."

His slim figure stepped out into the light and he asked, "How did you know it was me?"

Joan smirked. "You're not as good as you think. Enjoying the lights?"

"What, a guy can't go see Christmas lights by himself?" he asked innocently.

"It's a little sad unless you're here with someone: a kid, a date, a group of friends," she rattled off. "Plus, people coming here for the lights usually stick to the path. So what are you really doing here?"

"I'm here to ask you a favor," he replied truthfully.

Joan raised an inquisitive eyebrow. *That's different*. "You've got two minutes."

"I want you to train me. As an augmenter," he qualified.

"You know I can't do that," Joan answered dismissively. "Augmenters are born, not trained."

"Theoretically, what if one underwent something that could be considered a rebirth? Would it be possible to gain such abilities?" he framed it as a hypothetical.

Joan shifted her weight to one hip and bit her lip in

thought. "Theoretically, it's possible…but I'm more familiar with the doing and less with the theory. Have you reported it?"

"I haven't filed my final case report yet," he admitted. "I kinda wanted to check with you first."

"To see if I would help?" Liu guessed.

"To give you the courtesy of saying no if you didn't want to. There's a good chance Leader would have ordered you to do it if I did it the other way around." His answer seemed sincere and it took her by surprise. It struck her as both very considerate and un-Wilson-like.

"And what do I get out of it?" Joan asked.

"What do you want?" Wilson opened the floor for negotiations. Joan Liu—codename Aurora—was undoubtedly the best augmenter he had come across.

"Tit for tat. I train you in augmentation, you train me in summoning," Joan bargained.

Wilson gave her an appraising stare. "I never knew you had an interest," he responded.

"That's because you never asked," she said pointedly. "Do we have a deal?" She extended her hand and just a thread of her will.

Wilson reached for both with his own. "Yeah, we have a deal." The arcane spark of an agreement made crackled amidst the twinkling lights.

Joan nodded. "I've got to go and get some hot chocolate; message me and we'll figure out a schedule later. But for now, stop slinking in the shadows and enjoy the lights."

THE END

The agents of The Salt Mine will return in *Bone Dry*

Printed in Great Britain
by Amazon